A Tapestry of Colours 2

Stories from Asia

Edited by

Anitha Devi Pillai

Marshall Cavendish
Editions

Published by Marshall Cavendish Editions
An imprint of Marshall Cavendish International

A member of the
Times Publishing Group

Other Marshall Cavendish Offices:
Marshall Cavendish Corporation, 800 Westchester Ave, Suite N-641, Rye Brook, NY 10573, USA • Marshall Cavendish International (Thailand) Co Ltd, 253 Asoke, 16th Floor, Sukhumvit 21 Road, Klongtoey Nua, Wattana, Bangkok 10110, Thailand • Marshall Cavendish (Malaysia) Sdn Bhd, Times Subang, Lot 46, Subang Hi-Tech Industrial Park, Batu Tiga, 40000 Shah Alam, Selangor Darul Ehsan, Malaysia

National Library Board, Singapore Cataloguing in Publication Data

Title: A tapestry of colours. 2 : stories from Asia / Edited by Anitha Devi Pillai.
Description: Singapore : Marshall Cavendish Editions, [2021]
Identifiers: OCN 1247399953 | ISBN 978-981-4928-73-1
Subjects: LCSH: Short stories, English—Asia. | Short stories, Singaporean (English)
Classification: DDC 823.0108—dc23

Printed in Singapore

Cover image: Shutterstock, by Marukopum

Contents

Foreword

The two-volume set of *A Tapestry of Colours – Stories from Asia*, edited by Dr Anitha Devi Pillai, offers teachers a uniquely valuable resource for classrooms and an extraordinary opportunity to help students discover for themselves what the reading of literature can offer to them in delight and in their expanded understanding of human experience. Of all the literary genres, the genre of the short story seems to me most suitable for classroom use. Short stories are, by definition, fiction that can be read in what used to be called "one sitting." I love the idea of a "sitting," and recently saw it defined as 20 minutes to an hour. In my own years as an elementary and secondary student, 20 minutes may have been the outer limit of my capacity to sit in one place. But a good story might hold me somewhat longer, and the stories in this volume promise to hold students long enough to be read, if not always in one sitting, surely in no more than two sittings and usually well within the time typically allotted in a classroom both for reading and for discussion of what was read.

The individual stories in these two volumes, moreover, are presented in a textual setting that is likely to promote and deepen the reflection and discussion that inevitably follows classroom reading – and certainly ought to follow reading, if students are to gain the full benefit from what they have read. The setting I am referring to for these stories is the apparatus provided in these volumes for every included story, whereby each story is prefaced by a short personal note from its writer about the cultural context in which the story was written, and followed by the writer's account of how the completed story came into being: what occasioned it, what problems it presented, what the writer was hoping to accomplish for the reader and so on. The effect of this framing material is, first, to enhance a reader's interest in the story, based on the reader's intensified sense of personal involvement with the writer, and second, to deepen a reader's understanding of the story, by ensuring that the reader understands the cultural references or historical moment, or personal circumstances that are the context for each individual story and writer.

We must remember that short stories are not specialized technical kinds of discourse (though they can take on new and unfamiliar forms and include entirely original features), but they represent the literary genre that is most natural to all human beings in every human society. They have their anthropological origins in dreams and gossip and myths and family adventures and personal experiences that are told in everyday life and are frequently worth re-telling. Every child and adult knows from living with other human beings how to listen to and respond to such stories. As teachers of literary short stories, we must build on rather than cancel out the competence of all our students as persons with extensive experience in hearing and enjoying stories.

And, given the excellent collection of stories presented here, with their illuminating introductions and intimate accounts of their generative occasions, almost no student will be able to resist the essential dimension of literary experience – that of becoming immersed in the story itself and thereby ready for rich conversation about what happened and why we care.

Sheridan Blau, PhD
Professor of Practice in the Teaching of English
Department of Arts and Humanities
Teachers College, Columbia University;
Emeritus Professor of English and Education
University of California, Santa Barbara

Preface

The short story is a very welcoming text type as its brevity and accessibility make it an excellent platform to explore unknown topics and difficult subjects. It also gives readers an insight into other worlds and lives of people across the world within a short period of time.

In fact, short story readers were found to be more thoughtful, creative and willing to consider competing viewpoints than non-fictional essay readers by Maja Djikic, Keith Oatley and Mihnea Moldoveanu from the University of Toronto. Short story readers were also found to be open to exploring unfamiliar territories which helped to broaden their minds and engage them in honest conversations about the lives and actions of others. In other words, short stories have been found to be effective in nurturing empathetic readers who are respectful of other cultures. As the prolific author Neil Gaiman once said, "Fiction gives us empathy: it puts us inside the minds of other people, gives us the gifts of seeing the world through their eyes."

These two collections of short stories, *A Tapestry of Colours 1 & 2 – Stories from Asia*, aim to do just that by presenting stories from our neighbours in Asia and providing us with a means to understand them through narratives. This makes these collections of stories a valuable resource in the language and literature classroom as well.

Emeritus Professor Sheridan Blau, a well-renowned academic of English and Education at Teacher's College, Columbia University, illuminates the unique nature of these two books, which connects each short story to its setting and the writer and the importance of doing so. I am deeply grateful that Professor

Blau's insightful comments captured the essence of the value of short stories to readers.

The contributing writers have captured the spirit and multiple facets of living and growing up in various parts of Asia (Singapore, Malaysia, Thailand, Philippines, Indonesia, China, Korea, Japan, Bangladesh and India). The writers have to be commended for their collective willingness to share notes on their craft as they add an important perspective. I am indebted to the writers for their support and am deeply grateful to them for helping to create a meaningful conversation about the different facets of Asia.

I am also grateful to the following educators and passionate fiction lovers who have helped to provide comments on the short stories to make them very relatable and meaningful for youths: Aileen Chai, Amanda Sarah Chin, Amala Rajan, Azeena Badarudeen, Bernice Xu, Geetha Creffield, John Praveen Raj, Dr Mary Ellis, Michelle Wong, Priyanka Chakraborty, Selvarani Suppiah, Shafiq Rafi, Shalini Damodaran and Tivona Low.

Special thanks to Sumi Baby Thomas, the research assistant on this project.

Last but not least, I would like to thank the publishing team from Marshall Cavendish International: Melvin Neo, Mindy Pang and Anita Teo for bringing this set of books to life and to the public.

Anitha Devi Pillai

Newspaper Phantom

Clara Mok

Singaporeans would remember waking up to the "plop" of newspapers landing on their doorsteps or the sight of folded newspapers tucked between the grilles of their flat gates. In private estates, some newspapers land right on target under covered porches, while some land in the open. A heavy rain would result in the newspapers in the open getting drenched and soggy, and would have to be replaced by the newspaper vendor.

Most Singaporeans may have never come face to face with their newspaper carriers. The only evidence of their phantom-like existence would be the newspapers at their doorsteps. Newspaper delivery usually starts at 3am and ends around 6am. The rationale for the early timing is to enable subscribers to read the newspaper over breakfast.

Unfortunately, newspaper delivery service is a fast-disappearing trade in Singapore as more subscribers prefer to read their newspapers online. There are now even newspaper vending machines placed at strategic locations. Nevertheless, newspaper vendors and carriers are part of Singapore's cultural heritage, etched in the hearts and minds of older Singaporeans.

Pitch dark, 3.30am. Bleary-eyed 50-year-old Siok pushed a trolley towards a white minivan parked along the side of the road. Under dimly lit street lamps, its boot opened to reveal newspapers stacked neatly in bundles right up to the roof of the vehicle.

Jason handed her a disproportionately thick stack of newspapers and Siok grimaced under the sheer weight of the stack. With a frayed pair of gloves blackened with newspaper ink, she fingered the stack and drew out exactly 50 copies of *The Nation Times*, 30 copies of *Jishi Zaobao* and 10 copies of *Malay Express,* piling them on her trolley.

The early morning chill attacked her emaciated body. In the still of the pre-dawn morning, her footsteps pounded on the tar soundlessly, leaving no traces except for the soft landing of newspapers on the elongated front porches of the terrace houses.

Through her ten years of plying the Pasir Ris Green Estate route, she knew the exact angle and strength to toss the papers. Too hard and they were wedged on the window ledges. Too soft and they landed near the gates, or worse, on the lawns, heightening the risk of her precious commodity getting ravaged by early morning showers. Either way, she was prepared for an onslaught of complaints, and an inevitable reprimand from Jason. "I'm doing this for my son. I must bear it," she thought.

Once, a full-grown German shepherd broke from its leash and bounded after her. With the fang-baring beast snapping at her shins, she dropped the newspapers and fled a few streets away until its owner whistled and the dog gave up its chase. By then, she was shaking so hard that she collapsed on the asphalt, breathing in rapid bursts, her face drained of colour. Afterwards, Siok got an earful from Jason.

She refused to succumb to tears. She had not cried when her doctor informed her of her bad knee, or when she lost her job as a dishwasher, or when her husband ran away with another woman, so she was not about to cry over a dumb dog. Instead of a head-on clash with Jason, she turned vegetarian and prayed at the temple every first and fifteenth of the month for blessings on Wei's studies and her job.

Whenever it rained, she unfolded a huge piece of tarpaulin and spread it over the newspapers. Siok herself was not spared the torrents, pelting on her gaunt frame. At the end of a thunderstorm, her straggly white hair dripped like a wet mop. When asked, she would shrug, "What to do? I have to make a living. I want to send my son to university." Her newspaper round ended around 5am, in time for her to rush home to help her son get ready for school. Back home, Siok sat on her sofa and took a deep breath.

She meant to take only a quick nap. Her body, having taken a toll of consecutive days without proper rest, had eased into a deep slumber. Siok jerked awake on the sofa. She blinked at the intensity of the light invading her two-bedroom HDB flat. Through the thin worn-out curtains, light bounced off the white streaks of her hair. She glanced at the lone clock on the wall. Oh no, it's 7am, only 15 minutes to get ready! Thank goodness the school was just a ten-minute walk away. She lowered her aching feet into a pair of cheap plastic sandals.

Her 15-year-old was still fast asleep. Her knees creaked as her thin sandals dragged against the cold ceramic tiles.

"Wei! Wake up! Time for school!" Siok called out as she flicked on his room light.

Wei groaned on his bed. His eyes refused to open.

"Hurry up, late already!" urged Siok, shaking him.

"Mmm …!" Wei made a guttural sound.

"Come on! It's 7.30!"

"What?" Wei propped himself up, his eyes sharp and accusing.

"Mah, why didn't you wake me up earlier? I'm late!" Wei shouted as he jumped out of bed.

"But Mah, it's 7, not 7.30!" he protested, pointing at the clock in the living room.

Siok shook her head and shuffled to the kitchen to warm up the multigrain porridge. Siok's stomach growled as she opened the refrigerator to take out ground black sesame and sprinkled them over the porridge. Then she poured freshly boiled water into a porcelain cup with Milo powder and stirred with a metal spoon. The spoon clinked on the sides of the cup in protest. With her forehead throbbing, she tottered towards the dining table with the bowl of porridge and cup of Milo balanced in her hands.

Wei was tugging on the second sleeve of his uniform shirt, threatening to tear it at the armpit, his face taut.

"Eat your breakfast before you go!"

"Mah, I'm late!" Wei grumbled.

"Drink the Milo."

"Mah, the discipline master will scold me. I'll eat during recess. Bye!"

Lifting his bag, Wei whizzed out of the house.

"Hey …" Siok's voice trailed after Wei. She stretched out her hand to pass him his water bottle as he brushed past her. The brusque shutting of the front gate sent a jolt to her heart.

"That boy!" she wailed, wiping off her tears with the back of her wrinkled hand. "I'll teach him a lesson when he comes back."

She let out a big sigh at the untouched porridge and Milo on the table. She brought the porcelain cup to her lips and let the warm beverage slide down her throat. "What a waste. Ah, I can keep the porridge for Wei when he comes home after basketball."

Dabbing medicinal ointment to her temples to drive away the pounding headache, she sat on the sofa, letting her mind wander. Her eyes landed on Wei's kindergarten graduation photograph on the television console. Siok's face brightened as she contemplated an image in her mind of a mortarboard on Wei's head and a scroll in his hands upon his graduation from university, the culmination of her hopes and dreams for her only child. "Wei, he's so smart! I wish he could be a doctor or lawyer."

The toils of her unconventional hours of work had sapped her youthfulness away. She could even pass for a 70-year-old, so she avoided looking into mirrors. Photographs of her were sorely missing from the row of framed pictures featuring Wei – when he was a baby, when he was taking his first steps, when he was holding his Primary School Leaving Certificate and when he was taking part in a basketball tournament.

Siok's primary school education and poor grasp of English had limited her job options. She was a cashier, dishwasher, packer and gardener before landing her newspaper delivery job. With more turning to news on the Internet, the demand for her delivery services had shrunk by more than half. As she pondered how she could afford Wei's secondary school uniform, books plus English tuition, a crushing pain pulsated and she rubbed her temples in slow circular motions to dispel a vicious headache. She set the alarm clock for 2pm, in time to start preparing lunch for Wei. Soon, her body melted into the sofa and gave in to drowsiness as lethargy consumed her in disturbed sleep.

After lunch, Wei sat at the dining table revising his schoolwork while Siok hammered her head repeatedly with her fists.

"Mah, stop that!"

"Wei, Mah's having a headache. Help me with my newspaper run tomorrow morning."

"Tomorrow is a school holiday. I don't want to wake up so early!" Wei protested.

"I'll give you $20."

"Deal!" Wei's face lit up at the thought that he could finally get his hands on the latest game. During recess, he could only stand aside as he watched his classmates battle one another online.

He could not help cursing internally when his mother shook him awake at 3am and she herself returned to bed. Rubbing his eyes, he dragged his feet as he headed out with the trolley in the early morning. "For the sake of my game …" He kept his mother's torn knitted work gloves in the pocket of his bermudas, disgusted at their resemblance to a granny's and thought that they did not fit his manly image. Yet, his mother had insisted that he brought them with him. He was afraid that he might bump into friends from school. "They'll make me a laughing stock!" Wei thought.

He made long strides as he crossed the road over to Jason's minivan.

"Who are you?" asked Jason.

"Siok … my mum is not well. I'm here to replace her," said Wei, as he shifted his weight from one foot to the other. Jason stared at Wei for a while before handing him the stack. "You know the route, young man?" he said, patting his back. "I don't want any complaints." Wei knew better than to argue with him. He simply nodded and told himself, "I'll just do my job and head home to sleep."

Clutching a piece of paper that his mother had sketched for him, he could tell, from a series of crosses and alphabets showing designated houses, where the newspapers should be delivered. After covering two streets, Wei gained momentum in his first solo morning newspaper run.

While tossing a newspaper to a corner terrace house, it landed smack on a black mongrel, awakening it from slumber. It growled at him through the fence with the ferocity of a tiger baring its fangs, shattering the peace of the neighbourhood. "What the …" he cursed. His heartbeat escalated. Recalling his mother's close encounter with a dog, Wei's first instinct was to run home and hide under the security of his snug blanket. An image of his mother lying down at home, incapacitated, tugged at him when he broke into a run. No matter how hard he shook off the image, it refused to go away.

"I must get my money!" Wei said, and willed himself to turn back to where he had left his trolley. A cold draft yanked the remaining newspapers off his trolley and a few lifted off and flew in different directions. He scrambled after the papers, snatching them up in a frantic attempt to salvage them. The wind sent the first drops of drizzle right onto his precious commodity. He struggled to cover them with the tarpaulin and to secure the whole pile as leaves rustled briskly and tree branches bent over like old men.

"No time to waste!" he thought. His stack disappeared from his trolley at record speed. Luckily, he was one step ahead in finishing his deliveries before the rain poured with a vengeance. Dripping wet, he squatted in a corner in the five-foot way of a shophouse. Shivering lightly in his T-shirt, he dipped into his pockets for warmth and took comfort in his mother's knitted gloves. He took them out, slipped them over his hands and stared at the worn-out threads sticking out of the gloves. A heavy solemnity descended upon him as he wondered how long this pair of gloves would last. As he attempted to stand up, his arm and leg muscles contracted in spasms. He could not imagine how his 50-year-old mother managed to withstand the hardship for so many years without rest days.

"Mah, I will be the man of the house," he had vowed after his father deserted them when he was ten. "I'll protect you." However, as he grew up, winning at video games became more important than keeping his promise to his mother.

"I'll buy breakfast for Mah," he said, shaking off thoughts of his mother's ill health and thumbed the miserable $2 note in his wallet. When the rain reduced to a drizzle, he dashed to the nearby market to buy his mother's favourite breakfast.

"Mah, your *chee cheong fun*!"[1] he said, as he gently nudged his mother awake.

"Oh! How did the newspaper run go?"

"Jason hardly asked me any questions before he passed me the newspapers. Lucky you passed me the list, or else …" Wei replied.

"It rained just now?"

"Yes, but I finished before that."

"Are you sure you didn't leave any newspapers out in the rain?"

"Don't worry, Mah!"

1 Steamed rice rolls, usually served with a sweet sauce or sesame oil and light soya sauce.

Wei and Siok sat down and tucked into the *chee cheong fun* in companionable silence.

"Mah, I'll go again tomorrow," Wei offered.

Siok recalled the many times she had refrained from asking Wei to help her. She could not believe her ears. "Really?"

"*Err* … I want pocket money to buy games."

"Is that all you can think about?" Siok said, her voice strained, her lips quivering.

For the first time, Wei looked at his ageing mother and saw her straggling white hair and the crows' feet under her eyes. He remembered her being hurt. He also realised that she had not been smiling or laughing much and he wanted that back.

"All I can think of are my stupid games!" he muttered in self-reproach. "Never think of Mah!" During the recent school holidays, he had asked his mother for permission to take up a part-time job in a fast food restaurant.

"I want to help you earn money," Wei insisted.

"Wei, I earn enough money for you. You don't worry."

"But my classmate also works there."

"You focus on your studies and go to university. You can take care of me after you finish university and get a good job."

"I get a good job but at what cost? I don't want you to fall sick!" he had blurted out.

Wei reached out to Siok's bony fingers and noted the warmth in her grip and the shine in her eyes. "Mah, I won't mention the games anymore. And, I'll help you with the newspaper delivery."

Author's Note

I was one of ten participants rushing to meet the two-week timeline to complete a given writing exercise of 1,000 words. This exercise eliminated any lingering thoughts of procrastination on my part as I pounded on my keyboard frantically to meet the deadline. As a writer, I am in awe of deadlines. I worship them like gods. They spur me to bring my writing to a crescendo. When I was stuck at the 600-word mark, a nudge from my fellow writers was all that I needed to meet the tight deadline before me.

The writing prompt for that week was "Writing a Slice of Life – Describe how a 35-year-old is preparing breakfast for the family". The prompt led me to think about the mother of one of my students. Her struggles as a newspaper delivery person had touched my heart. As a mother myself, I empathised with her determination to send her son to university and rooted for her as she put all her effort into her job. I visualised what the situation was like when she had to juggle her newspaper runs and make breakfast for her son.

I sought suggestions from fellow writers on how I could deepen the metaphor of the mother as a "phantom" – when she delivered newspapers and in the eyes of her son. One writer suggested erasing her from all her son's photographs. I found that suggestion quite clever, so I included it.

Having trusted writing friends to give encouragement and feedback is a blessing for any writer. I must admit that receiving negative feedback about my writing can be quite painful, and I may end up having to "kill" my darlings or edit out parts which I really love, but at the end of the day, I know that I will grow and emerge as a stronger writer.

Of *Cendol* and Truths

Carol Pang

After World War II, the British government started a process of decolonisation to grant independence to former colonies. This was largely because the colonies had become an expensive liability to the British government post-World War II.

In 1957, Malaya, under the leadership of Tunku Abdul Rahman, gained independence from the British. In 1961, Tunku Abdul Rahman proposed the merger of Malaya, Singapore, Sabah, Brunei and Sarawak to form Malaysia. It was believed that such a merger would counter the advancing threat of communism in Southeast Asia. The British supported this proposal. However, many people in Sarawak objected to joining the merger as they preferred self-governance and independence, fearing that the new federation would not have the best interests, economically and otherwise, of Sarawak at heart.

In August 1963, representatives from the United Nations arrived in Sarawak to obtain the views of the people on joining the Federation of Malaysia and concluded that the majority of the population had agreed to join Malaysia. The Federation of Malaysia – consisting of Malaya, Singapore, Sabah and Sarawak – was formed on 16 September 1963. In 1965, Singapore left the federation.

2020

"Please welcome Professor Chong Ee Lynn onto the stage. Professor Chong is a visiting professor of history at Sarawak University. She's here to talk about her new book, *Stories from the Sarawak Insurgency: 1963–1973*. Congratulations on your book, Professor."

"Thank you, Clarence. It's a dream come true, in a way. I've dreamt of becoming a writer since I was a young girl."

"So, Professor, what made you pursue a career in history instead?"

"You could say that my dreams of being a writer took a detour when … I met a very special young man." Ee Lynn gazed into the distance. "It was a long time ago. The year was 1961."

* * *

1961

Three sisters are spending a perfect summer day by the river. The eldest is a bossy 17-year-old called Sue Lynn, the youngest is a 13-year-old tomboy, Jing Lynn. And dear readers, I'm the 16-year-old middle sister. I love my hometown Kuching, my Pa, my sisters, yes, even the bossy …

"Oh … hey!" Ee Lynn snapped out of her thoughts to find herself writing in thin air. "Give it back, Sue Lynn!"

"What's this? 'A perfect summer day'?" Sue Lynn read out loud while Ee Lynn reached ineffectually for her notebook. "In case it's escaped your notice, there's no 'summer' here. It's either hot or raining. *All year round.*" Sue Lynn threw the notebook back at Ee Lynn. "Listen, aren't you sick of the weather? I can't wait to leave this place."

"Ee Lynn and I are going to England when we finish school. Aren't we, Ee Lynn?" Jing Lynn chipped in from her perch on a log. "Ee Lynn's going to be a writer. I'm going to be a doctor, like Pa."

"That's right." Ee Lynn eyed Sue Lynn warily. She could almost predict what her sister would say next.

"I don't know which of you is more ridiculous," Sue Lynn scoffed. "You, with your head in the clouds – how are you going to make a living as a writer? And you …" Sue Lynn turned around to Jing Lynn. "What the heck are you doing?"

"Learning to swim, of course." Jing Lynn was lying belly down on a fallen log. She was making vigorous arm and leg movements while following pictorial swimming instructions from a book she had propped up on the log.

"You know, Sue Lynn, it's none of your business what I do with my life," Ee Lynn said.

"Actually, I'm the eldest in the family, that makes it my business," Sue Lynn said.

"You're the oldest by only eleven months," Ee Lynn argued. "And in a way, it's better to float in the clouds than be obsessed by the *size* of a guy's wallet. It-it's unnatural!"

"It's called being realistic," Sue Lynn said.

"What about your plans, huh, Sue Lynn?" Ee Lynn asked. "What will you do now that Robert has dumped you for Cecile?"

"Robert and Cecile sitting in a tree, K-I-S-S-I-N-G," Jing Lynn chanted and made kissing noises.

"The two losers deserve each other," Sue Lynn scoffed.

"Oh, don't act so cool," Ee Lynn said. "I heard you crying in bed last week."

"Once you've been outside of this cesspool we call home, you'll find that the boys here are just mere tadpoles," Sue Lynn said.

Before Ee Lynn could think of a retort, Jing Lynn climbed off the log and walked over to her. Ee Lynn nodded at Jing Lynn. They then ran to Sue Lynn, grabbed hold of an arm each and dragged a screaming Sue Lynn into the river.

"My dress! It's ruined!" Sue Lynn shouted at her sisters.

"And your hair! It's like seaweed!" Jing Lynn started giggling.

Ee Lynn looked at Sue Lynn's muddy face and dress, and she too started laughing.

Sue Lynn tossed her hair behind her back and said, "Looks like you two monkeys have forgotten one important thing."

"Wh-what's that?" Jing Lynn asked in between her laughter.

"I'm the reigning water-fighting champion!" Sue Lynn lunged at Jing Lynn and tickled her. Ee Lynn splashed towards her sisters and joined in the game. The three of them were soon wet and hoarse from shouting and laughing.

* * *

Later that evening, the Chong family and their lodger, Han Long, were sitting at the dining table behind Chong's Clinic. The clinic occupied the front of the ground floor of a narrow and deep shophouse, with the dining room and kitchen situated behind the clinic. The first floor of the shophouse served as the family's living quarters.

"Why is dinner late today, Sue Lynn?" Chong asked.

"We were at the ri … *ouch*!" Jing Lynn yelped as Ee Lynn kicked her ankle under the dining table.

"Sorry, Pa," Sue Lynn said.

"You're the oldest, Sue Lynn," Chong said. "Your Ma is no longer with us. I rely on you to set a good example to your sisters."

"Yes, Pa," Sue Lynn said.

The dining room was momentarily quiet as everyone tucked into a meal of rice and dishes of ginger chicken, omelette and stir-fried Chinese cabbage.

"Han Long, who do you think is prettier? Sue Lynn or Ee Lynn?' Jing Lynn piped up suddenly. "Everyone says Sue Lynn is pretty but Ee Lynn is clever. Do you agree?"

Ee Lynn rolled her eyes and saw Sue Lynn glare at Jing Lynn. Han Long's face turned red and he started choking. Ee Lynn quickly filled his cup with Chinese tea and he put down his chopsticks and rice bowl to take a sip of tea.

"Ignore my youngest." Chong chuckled and ruffled Jing Lynn's hair.

"It-it's fine, Dr Chong," Han Long mumbled as he stared into his cup.

"How are things in Bau?" Chong asked Han Long.

"Things are getting worse." Han Long looked up at Chong. "They took our neighbour, Old Lim, in for questioning last week. They suspect he might be helping his son."

"Why shouldn't Old Lim help his son?" Jing Lynn demanded.

"Jing Lynn, be quiet." Sue Lynn shushed her sister. "You don't know anything."

"Your sister is right," Chong said. "These are complicated, very … well, complicated times. There are things you children don't understand."

"You should tell them," Han Long stated. "They're old enough."

"What'd you say?" Chong asked.

"These are dangerous times for Sarawak," Han Long said. "They want to tie us to Malaya. Do we want another foreign power to rule over Sarawak? The days of the imperialists are over. Look at India! And Gandhi!"

Ee Lynn watched in surprise as the red spots on Han Long's face began to colour again, this time from passion. She could tell from her father's expression that he had never seen this side of Han Long before either.

"Well, on the other hand, there are some who think Sarawak isn't ready for self-rule," Chong said mildly. "They think our society's inexperienced, we need safer hands."

"These are the people who'd hand over Sarawak, and all her riches to the Malayans," Han Long's voice rose in anger. "Can we trust others to be the best guardians of our oil, our rainforests? Can we trust others to look out for us? Our hands, our inexperienced hands, are the ones I trust."

"Enough!" Chong said forcefully. "Your parents wouldn't want to lose their son to the vagaries of politics. When you came here to study for your degree, your parents placed you under my care. I forbid you to get involved in politics. Is that clear?"

When Han Long finally looked down into his cup and muttered "Yes", Ee Lynn realised that she had been holding her breath while waiting for his answer.

* * *

When the United Nations (UN) team arrived in Kuching in 1963 to sample the opinion of Sarawakians on the proposed merger with Malaya, protesters lined the road from the airport to the town centre to demonstrate against the federation. The UN team faced similar protests in other cities, including Sibu and Miri.

The UN concluded that the majority of the population was in favour of the federation.

* * *

India Street, the bustling heart of Kuching, was flanked by two rows of shophouses selling everything from groceries and books to gold and jewellery.

"Isn't that Han Long?" Jing Lynn nudged Ee Lynn, as they walked out of Tai An grocery store with the week's shopping.

The two girls watched as Han Long looked left and right before entering Bright Lights bookshop.

"Take these home," Ee Lynn said as she handed the grocery bags to Jing Lynn. "I have to go to the bookshop."

"I want to go too," Jing Lynn whined.

"Sue Lynn is waiting for the groceries." Ee Lynn put her hands on her hips. "I'm older than you, so do as I say."

Jing Lynn left, grumbling as she did so.

In the bookshop, Ee Lynn spotted Han Long's six-foot-tall frame easily. He was browsing the Chinese literature shelves. She moved to a nearby aisle, taking care not to be seen by him. She heard some whispering, and peered through the books to see who he was talking to. His aisle was empty except for a girl who was leaving.

Ee Lynn jumped as someone tapped her on her shoulder. She wheeled around to see the puzzled-looking face of Han Long.

"The best football teams in World Cup history?" Han Long read the title of the book that Ee Lynn had grabbed hurriedly from a shelf.

"Um, my teachers think I should, er, expand my horizon, develop new interests." Ee Lynn shoved the book back onto the shelf.

"Were you following me?"

"Oh uh … what?" Ee Lynn's eyes widened as she feigned innocence.

"Spying on me, perhaps?"

"No! Why? Do you have something to hide?"

"Why would you think that?"

"No reason. But, who's the girl you were talking to?"

"You really want to know?" Han Long leaned down towards Ee Lynn and smiled cheekily.

"Um, er …" Ee Lynn felt herself getting flustered.

"Come. I'll show you." Han Long took Ee Lynn's wrist and led her out of the bookshop. He unchained his bike from a railing outside the shop.

"I assume you walked here?" Han Long asked. Ee Lynn nodded. "You can ride on the back. Hop on."

"Where are we going?"

"You'll see."

* * *

"This *cendol* is delicious!" Ee Lynn shuddered as she experienced a brain freeze. She had just swallowed a large spoonful of the shaved-ice dessert topped with green jelly and coconut milk. "How do you know about this place?" They were sitting by the side of a narrow lane that ran between a Chinese temple and a church.

"Do you remember me talking about Old Lim the other night?" Han Long asked.

Ee Lynn nodded.

Han Long continued, "Old Lim's son, Ah Onn, was my classmate. Our class raised some money to help with Old Lim's legal fees. To answer your question at the bookshop, that girl I met at the bookshop was giving me the money our class has collected." Han Long gestured towards the woman who ran the *cendol* stall. "Ming is Ah Onn's sister. I've just passed the money to her. Coincidentally, Ming's husband runs the noodle stall next to her. He makes the best laksa in town."

"You sure like your food." Ee Lynn smiled.

Han Long patted his tummy. "Hey, I'm a growing boy."

Ee Lynn laughed. "You know, you're not like how you are at home."

"How am I at home?"

Ee Lynn thought for a moment. "Serious. Proper, in a way. Angry when you talk about Old Lim and … politics."

"Boring, you mean. And how am I now?"

"Young, carefree … almost."

"I'll take that as almost a compliment. So, tell me, what will you do after you've finished school?"

"I'm going to be a writer."

"A noble profession. Do you write much?"

"All the time, in my notebook. But that's private. Or about as private as it can be, with two sisters. What about you? Will you be an engineer after you graduate?"

"That's the plan. I like the idea of building things that'll last."

* * *

Is this how it feels to be in love? Exhilarated one moment, terrified the next, for how can our love burn at this intensity forever? Han Long is perfect. Smart, bold and funny. And he loves me! I'm sure of it.

Over the last few weeks, I would cycle to the university library after school and study with him. Afterwards, we would sit at the cendol stall and just talk. He doesn't treat me as the silly, impractical girl that Sue Lynn thinks I am. He listens to my thoughts. He values my opinions. He believes in my dreams, perhaps more strongly than even I believe in them.

Knowing him has changed how I see the world. I can now see my place in the world. I'm ready to become a woman. I'm ready to take the next step. I want to experience absolutely everything with the man that I love!

* * *

Advocates for Sarawak's independence included political party supporters, university students and secondary school students. Many of these political activists were from the Chinese community; they were mostly Chinese-educated with family ties in China.

The advancing threat of communism under Chairman Mao's China had impelled the British to support the creation of the Federation of Malaysia and to describe Sarawakians from the Chinese community who opposed the federation as communists.

* * *

Ee Lynn's face burned as she cycled through the town centre. Sue Lynn had no right! None! How dare she? Tears of anger pricked her eyes as she remembered how Pa had threatened to throw Han Long out of the house. Her calm, reasonable Pa. She had never seen him act so dementedly. And what would Han Long think? She had to speak to him before he heard it from anyone else.

* * *

"What are you doing here, Ee Lynn?" Han Long asked.

Ee Lynn had found Han Long at the university library and asked him to step outside.

"Oh, Han Long, I have to speak to you."

"What's wrong? Has something happened to your family?"

"No-no, they're fine."

"Here," Han Long walked over to an empty bench and gestured for Ee Lynn to sit beside him. "So, what is it?"

"I've done something terrible. Promise you won't be angry with me."

"What is it?"

"I can't tell you unless you promise."

"Ok, I promise."

"You know my notebook?"

"Yes?"

"Sue Lynn read it and she told Pa … she told Pa that we are, um, together. And Pa, he was angry and he wanted to throw you out of the house."

"Wh-what are you talking about?" Han Long asked, his brow furrowing.

"Of course, I ah, told them it isn't true, you know," Ee Lynn said, feeling a flush creep up her neck.

"Because … it's not?"

"Yes, so anyway, just so you know."

"So, we're not together? And I won't be thrown out of the house?" Han Long asked, still looking mildly confused.

"Yes. I mean, no," Ee Lynn blinked as she groped for the right words. "I mean, you're fine." Ee Lynn nodded her head at Han Long in what she hoped was a reassuring gesture.

"Why would Sue Lynn think that we are, er, together?"

"You could say it's because of what I wrote in my notebook. I wrote about us hanging out – which we did. But I also wrote about things that we haven't done, uh, did not do, I mean, will not do. It's fiction … that's what I write, fiction." Ee Lynn finished in a rush, looking down at the floor and wishing it would swallow her up.

Han Long laughed. "And you were worried about this?"

"I'm so sorry. I didn't mean to get you into trouble."

Han Long laughed even harder and patted Ee Lynn's shoulder. "Oh, you silly girl."

"So, you're not angry?" Ee Lynn looked up at Han Long's laughter.

"No! It's the most amusing thing I've heard in ages."

"Wait … are you laughing at me?"

"I'm laughing because these are trivial things."

"It took a lot of courage for me to tell you this," Ee Lynn admitted in a small voice.

"We live in dark times right now, Ee Lynn. Our friends, neighbours and classmates are disappearing daily. But you're concerned with fiction and stories?"

"You said that writing was a noble profession," Ee Lynn half-whispered through her increasingly constricted throat.

"There are times when even writers have to choose what to do with their pens. Will you continue to hide behind Daddy's wings? Or will you fight for what you believe in?"

Ee Lynn felt tears threaten for the second time that afternoon. She tried to stare back at Han Long but she had to break off her eye contact to blink back her tears before they fell.

* * *

To him, I'm merely a child. He doesn't see me as his equal. He doesn't love me. It was all me! And yet, this ache in my heart is real. I'm so sad! Though not as sad as when Ma died. Oh, I want Ma! I never want to leave this room and see anyone. I know, I'll ask Jing Lynn to bring me food so I won't have to leave the room.

"Jing Lynn, is that you?' Ee Lynn sniffed from under her blanket.

"Why are you crying?" Jing Lynn asked softly.

"Han Long, he-he doesn't love me."

"I thought he's your friend, our friend."

"He is. I-I thought he loved me. But he doesn't! He only cares about his stupid politics! Independence, self-rule … rubbish!"

"If he makes you sad, you should tell Pa. Or the police," Jing Lynn said.

"I can't do that."

"I can."

"No, don't say anything," Ee Lynn gripped Jing Lynn's arm. "Promise me, Jing Lynn."

"OK. Just stop … being sad," Jing Lynn said, patting Ee Lynn on her arm awkwardly.

* * *

Activists who organised and protested against joining the Federation of Malaysia were targeted for arrests. Some were exiled to China.

The wider community regarded a prisoner who disclosed the names of others in the movement against the federation as a traitor.

* * *

In the weeks after Ee Lynn had cried about the end of her fantasised relationship with Han Long, she went home late by studying at the school library or at her friend, Selma's place. This way, she could avoid seeing Han Long, and well, out of sight, out of mind … eventually, she hoped.

One afternoon, just as Ee Lynn was heading to the library after her classes, a girl ran towards her, panting. It took a moment for Ee Lynn to recognise her – she was Han Long's classmate, the girl from Bright Lights bookshop.

"Ee Lynn, you're Ee Lynn. Han Long's your lodger, right?" the girl sputtered.

Ee Lynn nodded in confusion, "Yeah, wh-what's going on?"

"Han Long …" the girl took a deep breath and started again. "We heard that your sister, Jing Lynn, has gone to the police. She told the police, um, stuff about Han Long."

"Jing Lynn? Our Jing Lynn? What are you talking about?"

"She … we don't know what she's told the police. But we have to warn Han Long. Han Long told me you are friends. I know he trusts you. And right now, I have no choice but to trust you, too. Please, I can't go to him to warn him – there are eyes on me. So please, warn him, tell him to leave, now. Right now, you're the only one who can save him."

* * *

The quickest route from St Margaret's Secondary School to Chong's Clinic in Kuching town centre was via Saga Hill. Ee Lynn pedalled as hard as she could up the hill. She breathed in the stale, humid air and tasted the tangy beads of sweat that dripped off her nose. She ignored the mosquitoes that buzzed in her ear and attacked her exposed flesh.

She had taken this route hundreds of times before to get home from school. She knew that after a sharp hairpin turn at the top of the hill, a freewheeling descent would deliver the sweet relief of a breeze and, more importantly, speed.

What has she done? *Click-click!* What has Jing Lynn done? The unwelcome question reverberated through Ee Lynn's head in time to the circular motion of her pedals. When she finally reached the top of the hill, she spotted some stray rocks in her path but braked a second too late.

A moment later, she crashed and landed amongst the rocks and weeds by the side of the lane. Her vision was clouded by tears of pain as she bit her lip to stop herself from crying. She checked that she had not broken anything and climbed back onto her bike. Han Long had no time for her to stop and cry. She had to get back and warn him. She no longer cared about her hurt feelings and bruised ego. Please, just let him be safe.

* * *

Dusty and sweaty from her hurried ride home from school, Ee Lynn rushed into the living quarters above Chong's Clinic calling for Han Long. She came to a sudden halt as she took in the scene in the living room. Her Pa, Sue Lynn and Jing Lynn were standing in the middle of the room. They were all looking towards the bedrooms and none of them dared look in the direction of the armed policeman who stood next to Jing Lynn. Another policeman came out of Han Long's room and saw Ee Lynn.

"Who's this?" the second policeman asked.

"Ah, this is my second daughter, Inspector," Chong said.

"You were calling for this Han Long. Do you know where he is?" the police inspector asked Ee Lynn.

Ee Lynn tried to speak and no sound came out. She gulped and tried again. "No."

"Why were you looking for him?"

"I, uh, wanted his help with my, uh, maths homework,' Ee Lynn replied, saying the first thing that came to her mind.

The police inspector stared hard at Ee Lynn. After what felt like ages during which Ee Lynn tried to maintain an impassive face, the police inspector handed Chong a card. "If you hear from Han Long, ask him to call me at this number. We need to ask him a few questions."

"Of course, Inspector," Chong said. "Let me show you out."

* * *

"We were so nervous when the police arrived, weren't we, Sue Lynn?" Jing Lynn told Ee Lynn after the police left. "Pa told us to say nothing and to behave calmly."

"When you ran in shouting for Han Long, I thought you'd ruin everything." Sue Lynn gestured at Ee Lynn's scraped knees. "What happened? You're bleeding."

"Oh, it's nothing. I fell off my bike on Saga Hill." Ee Lynn crouched down to face Jing Lynn and held her shoulders. "Jing Lynn, did you go to the police?"

"Yes."

"I knew it! But, why?"

"I went to report Han Long."

"What have you done? Oh, what have you done?" Ee Lynn wailed and shook Jing Lynn's shoulders.

"Calm yourself, Ee Lynn!" Sue Lynn pulled Ee Lynn away from Jing Lynn.

Ee Lynn took a few deep breaths and asked, "What did you tell the police, Jing Lynn?"

"I told them, Han Long is a political activist. They asked me why I was reporting him. I said he made you sad."

"Oh Jing Lynn, I was sad. But that was weeks ago! What else did you tell them?" Ee Lynn asked Jing Lynn urgently.

"They asked me where he is. I said he'll be at the university library."

"Wait – it's Friday. Han Long doesn't go to the library on Fridays. He goes back to Bau for the weekend," Ee Lynn said, looking at Jing Lynn in confusion.

"Yes, he does," Chong said. Ee Lynn turned around to see that Chong had re-entered the living room.

Chong sank down into an armchair. "Han Long came to me last night. The police have arrested two of his classmates. He knows he'll be next. He asked me to buy him some time. So, I sent Jing Lynn to make a false police report. I thought the police were more likely to believe Jing Lynn, given her tender age."

"But Pa, I thought you didn't want us to get involved in politics," Ee Lynn said. "Why did you help Han Long?"

"Because it's not right." Chong rubbed his face. Ee Lynn thought that her Pa had aged overnight. "Our young people should not be arrested for their political views. Han Long deserves to have a future."

"Why didn't you tell me?" Ee Lynn protested.

"You were studying at your friend, Selma's place last night," Chong replied. "We didn't have time."

"Where's Han Long now?" Ee Lynn asked.

"He thought it best if we didn't know where he went." Chong took out a letter from his wallet and handed it to Ee Lynn. "He asked me to give you this."

"Listen, Ee Lynn, Jing Lynn, go pack your things," Sue Lynn said. "We're leaving in the morning."

"Leaving? Where? Why?" Ee Lynn asked in bafflement.

"We can't stay in Sarawak," Sue Lynn said. "What will happen when the police find out about the false report?"

"But to leave Kuching!" Ee Lynn exclaimed. "What about school?"

"You girls will stay with your Aunty May in London," Chong said. "You'll continue your schooling there."

"I, for one, can't wait to leave Kuching," Sue Lynn declared. "It's such a small, suffocating place. Everyone knows you and has an opinion on everything that you do."

"Like the boy in the bookshop who always notices when you've had a haircut," Ee Lynn said, looking at Sue Lynn with tears in her eyes.

"Or the aunty in the market who always gives you extra pancakes, because she wants you to tutor her son," Sue Lynn choked out at Ee Lynn, her voice breaking.

"I'll miss St Margaret's. The teachers are nice." Jing Lynn reached out and held Ee Lynn's hand tightly. "Do you think my friends will go swimming in the river without me?"

"We'll return." Ee Lynn hugged a sobbing Jing Lynn. "We will, one day." Chong and Sue Lynn gathered around Ee Lynn and Jing Lynn, and they clung on to each other for a long time.

* * *

The activists who opposed Sarawak joining the Federation of Malaysia met various fates - some were arrested, some left for other countries while others went into hiding to continue the resistance.

In 1973, the North Kalimantan resistance movement signed an agreement in Simanggang to end the insurgency. To commemorate the event, Simanggang was renamed Sri Aman, meaning a town of peace.

* * *

2020

"Professor? Professor?"

"Sorry, I was lost in my thoughts. Could you repeat the question, please?" Ee Lynn asked.

"Certainly. The question is, why did you decide to write this book?" Clarence repeated his question.

"As you know, Clarence, history isn't set in stone. In a way, history is constantly being refined, reinterpreted, even fought over. With this book, I hope to give voice to some of those whom history may have judged unkindly, so that their truths … are heard."

* * *

Dear Ee Lynn,

I'm sorry I won't get to see you before I leave. I know that I hurt you with what I said outside the library a few weeks ago. I'm sorry I spoke unthinkingly. I realise that my passion for the cause can sometimes make me hurt those that I care about, like my parents, and you.

I'm grateful for your friendship and laughter these past few months. Perhaps if we had met under different circumstances, we could have meant more to each other. But neither of us can afford to dwell on "what if's".

I hope that you'll achieve your dreams and that you'll one day be able to wield your pen in pursuit of your beliefs and truths. For those of us who can't do so, you must live. Live well. Live fully.

Yours,
Han Long

Author's Note

The biggest inspiration for my story, "Of *Cendol* and Truths", comes from my mother, a gifted oral storyteller of family tales – about her childhood, her siblings and what it was like to grow up in Kuching, Sarawak, Malaysia. I used *cendol* in the story and in the title as a tribute to my mother – it's one of her favourite desserts.

For the story, I conducted desktop research and interviewed people who lived through those historical times. However, this story is a work of fiction and isn't completely historically accurate. I made choices – between using historical facts and fiction – that I felt best served the story. For example, there wasn't actually a university in Kuching in the 1960s. However, I needed a reason for Han Long, a university student, to stay with the Chongs as a lodger. So, I made it up!

On the structure of the story, I tied the past to the present by framing the story with an opening scene and a penultimate scene, both of which feature an interview with the adult Ee Lynn in the present. By making the adult Ee Lynn a history professor, I could then insert historical extracts as if they are from her book about the Sarawak insurgency. By inserting extracts that are written in a factual style into a work of fiction, I hope to prompt readers into evaluating the truth of these "historical facts" and the accepted account of the Sarawak insurgency.

I further developed the theme of acknowledging different narratives of events or different truths by introducing echoes in a few instances. First, I foregrounded the plurality of "truths" in the story title. Second, in the penultimate scene, the adult Ee Lynn tells Clarence that she wants other voices and "their truths" to be heard. Third, in Han Long's letter to Ee Lynn, he encourages her to find her "truths".

With respect to style, I used some analogies to make my writing come alive. For example, in the river scene, Jing Lynn likens Sue Lynn's hair to seaweed and Sue Lynn describes the boys in Kuching as tadpoles, both of which are inspired by the river setting. The use of different media in the story – Ee Lynn's notebook extracts, extracts from Ee Lynn's book about the Sarawak insurgency and Han Long's letter to Ee Lynn – enables me to incorporate different points of view into the story.

Mrs Yip

Karen Kao

The Chinese Civil War began in earnest in 1945. The ruling Nationalist party, led by Chiang Kai-shek, battled with Mao Zedong and his communists for control over China. This was a land war where troops moved on foot from Manchuria in the north to Guangdong in the south, Peking in the east to Xinjiang in the west.

As the war dragged on, both sides needed more soldiers. The Communists wooed peasants with promises of land reform. When they conquered a city like Shanghai, their soldiers were not allowed to loot. Instead, they helped distribute rice rations. Both the Nationalists and the Communists used conscription to bolster their forces. Men (some elderly) and boys (some quite young) were forcibly taken from their towns and villages, factories and fields. Roped or chained together, they were marched off to war.

Mrs Yip adores life on the road. Can you hear the thump of her drum? All around her, sticks clatter to the ground. Soldiers fold their tents into green lozenges that slot neatly into their pack. Mrs Yip waits in line for the daily meal: a slab of rice that steams her metal bowl.

While she eats, scouts return with news of Nationalist nests. Guns click-clack all over the camp as soldiers load their weapons. Mrs Yip and the other women understand the signs. They hoist their bundles, ready to leave as soon as the bugle sounds.

It's been days since the last skirmish and the soldiers relish the prospect of a fight. Normally, the Nationalist troops run and why wouldn't they? Too many of them were taken from their farms and fishing boats to serve the tyrant, Chiang Kai-shek. Every day, dozens defect to the Red Army.

"Have you seen my husband?" Mrs Yip asks each new recruit. "What about my boy? He came up to my shoulder when he was taken away. Maybe now he's as tall as me."

She whistles a tune her boy would recognise. It was their signal that dinner was ready. He would always whistle the same tune back. So far, no one has answered.

So Mrs Yip marches on with a washtub on her head. This is her contribution to the cause: to wash socks and uniforms and the occasional slip of underwear left behind by a woman. Many women follow the army on its northward journey, now that victory is certain. Soon, Mao Zedong will sit on the Dragon Throne.

Mrs Yip aches to enter the Forbidden City. To set her straw sandals on a path where only emperors trod. The thought delights her so much that Mrs Yip must sing. Patriotic marches, lullabies, snippets from Cantonese opera and the dirty ditties that sprout from her memory. The other washerwomen giggle and clap as they wade through rice paddies, paddle across streams and climb karst mountains.

* * *

Peking still lies many months away when the rainy season arrives. Mrs Yip's straw sandals swell. Mould grows between her toes. All the silt in China accumulates at the bottom of her tub. Mrs Yip scrubs her fingers raw and still she cannot restore whiteness to the general's collar.

A sergeant comes to Mrs Yip's tent. He has the unwelcome task of marshalling the cooks and cleaners that service the troops. He says, "Go home, Mrs Yip. Your services as a washerwoman are no longer desired."

See the rain pelt Mrs Yip's head as she kowtows in the mud. Listen to her plaintive tones.

She reminds the sergeant that the other washerwomen are here for the money whereas she has a quest. “Besides,” Mrs Yip says, “I no longer have a home.”

The sergeant grants her petition but what a cost Mrs Yip must pay. As the Red Army liberates city after city, Mrs Yip's teeth chatter. The washerwomen donate blankets, clothes, whatever it takes to keep her warm. By the time the army reaches the banks of the Whangpoo River, a fever fells Mrs Yip. For three days and three nights, her skin burns.

On the fourth day, the army readies to leave. Mrs Yip begs the sergeant to wait. She asks for no favours. There's no need to carry her on a palanquin as if she were a Qing princess. She wouldn't even ride on the back of a supply truck. She would walk like any soldier for the sake of their common cause.

But the sergeant cannot hear her pleas. He won't enter her tent for fear of the disease inside. He gives the order to pack up. Soldiers fold her tent and remove her metal bowl. Her former friends, the washerwomen, come to blows over her washtub.

They abandon Mrs Yip in Shanghai with nothing more than a bedroll and the travel bundle that she tucks under her head.

* * *

Mrs Yip trawls the streets of Shanghai in search of work. On the Bund, she studies the banners that hang from the stone balconies. One banner promises total victory over Chiang Kai-shek. Another offers a cosmetic, guaranteed to whiten her skin. She reads every single one in the hope that someone will notice that she can.

But no one bothers with Mrs Yip. Look at her slumped by the foot of a bronze lion. Passers-by lean over her to rub the lion's nose. They say the gesture brings good luck but Mrs Yip is too tired to try. She rubs the paw instead. She takes off her straw hat to let the river breeze cool her face. For just a moment, she closes her eyes.

A coin drops into her hat. Mrs Yip's eyes open. The man before her wears a western suit with impeccably pressed trousers. He bends down to see her face. Mrs Yip smiles.

The man frowns. "No healthy worker needs to beg."

"I'm not begging."

"Your hat is on the ground."

"I was resting."

"You look like you're hungry," the man guesses. "And you have no work."

Mrs Yip has no snappy answer to that. She nods.

"What can you do?" the man asks.

Mrs Yip holds out her hands. Her palms are calloused. The back of her left hand bears the scar of an iron. Lye has caused the fingertips on her right hand to go white.

"Come with me," the man says.

The man owns a laundry. His name is Mr Bao. His laundry stands on a side street to the Quai de France.[1] The building has heavy wooden shutters and a red wooden door with a brass ring for a knocker.

A long key materialises out of Mr Bao's pocket. The door swings open to reveal a floor of wooden planks. As Mr Bao pushes back each shutter, new wonders appear. A counter with an abacus on top. Blue wrapping paper and twine on the shelves below. A wall of flat irons and a large vat of water over a freshly raked bed of coals. In the corner, a machine gleams green in the dim light.

"What is that?" Mrs Yip points.

Mr Bao beams. "It's a machine wringer. Imported from America."

"Where do I sleep?"

Mr Bao points to a narrow space between the wringer and the irons. "You can light a fire, if you like, to make tea."

---

1 Before 1949, Shanghai was divided into foreign concessions. The Quai de France ran through the French Concession and is now known as Zhongshan No 2 Road.

"Where do I find wood and water?"

Mr Bao plucks a key from a hook on the wall. The back door leads to an alley with a neat stack of firewood and a rain barrel.

"There are rats out here," Mr Bao warns. "Don't sleep with the door open. I'll be back tomorrow. Good night."

Mrs Yip paces her new home. It's smaller than the mud hut in Shenzhen but bigger than any tent. She spreads her bedroll its full length. She stores her travel bundle in the corner of a deep shelf.

In the morning, Mr Bao arrives with a pot of soup noodles tied to the back of his bicycle. He ladles out two full bowls. She places the pot under the bubbling wash tub. They eat together on the floor behind the counter.

Mrs Yip asks, "Who makes your food?"

"My wife," Mr Bao says proudly.

Mrs Bao is a terrible cook. No imagination and not enough salt. Look how thin the poor man is. Mrs Yip sees it every time a new load of sheets comes in. Then Mr Bao removes his elegant wool suit, his pristine white shirt and his leather wingtip shoes. He stores them in the back room where they can come to no harm. In nothing more than his singlet and a pair of baggy underpants, Mr Bao drops the sheets into the boiling water.

Mrs Yip won't risk the kind of scars that adorn Mr Bao's arms and legs. She protects herself with her horse blanket tied tightly around her middle. Only then will she plunge her stick in the steaming water to stir the sheets.

It takes two of them to lift the sheets out of the tub. Together, they hang them in the alley to dry.

Listen to the water clatter to the ground. See the rats flee.

* * *

Mrs Yip soon discovers others like her who live in this part of town. Some sleep under typesetting tables and others between silk looms. They are eager to sate her curiosity about life behind the Bund. Mr Bao's alley becomes their gathering place. They bring wooden crates to sit and food to share. Tea eggs, radish cakes and Mrs Yip's favourite salted plums.

At night, they gaze at the stars. They tell stories about the lovelorn milkmaid parted from her beloved weaver. They play drinking games with a sewing thimble and a bottle of *baijiu*.[2] Mrs Yip can't remember a time when she laughed so much.

The nights grow cold. Soon, they'll need to retreat indoors where new forms of amusement are required. They pool their money to buy a mahjong set and appoint one of them to procure the game.

The man returns with news from the French Concession. He reports, "The barbarians have gone mad. I saw a complete set of rosewood furniture for sale."

"How much money do they want?" Mrs Yip asks.

"The price of a ticket out of Shanghai."

Why would anyone want to leave such a beautiful place? When autumn ignites the trees, ducks speed like arrows down the Whangpoo River, headed for warmer climes. Shenzhen is warm. Shenzhen used to be home. But Mrs Yip no longer longs for the road. For the first time in many months, her belly is full.

One morning, she wakes to a commotion outside. Mrs Yip elbows her way through the crowd. A body emerges from the building, feet first.

"Who is it?" Mrs Yip asks.

A sheet hides the corpse from view. All she can see is a pair of yellow horned feet.

"It's Mr Bao," she keens. "I'd know those feet anywhere."

2 A clear, colourless liquor usually made from fermented sorghum.

"I'm standing right here," Mr Bao says, not unkindly.

Look how Mrs Yip blushes.

Mr Bao is so close that she can see that the nose hairs in his left nostril are longer than the right. Lucky for her that the sanitation workers distract Mr Bao's attention. The men drop the body into the back of a truck. The head slides down and the legs stick up like a pair of chopsticks in a bowl of rice. As the truck slowly moves away, the legs wave farewell. The crowd disperses and the work day begins.

A maid from one of the hotels on the Bund arrives to collect the sheets. A rickshaw driver deposits a bundle of soiled linen and clothing. When a barbarian appears at the counter, Mr Bao doesn't flinch.

Mrs Yip stares at the man from behind the flat irons. It's not as if she's never seen a barbarian before. Nuns from India taught her how to read and write. But they were as slight and finely built as Mrs Yip herself. This man jiggles with fat on all sides and his cheeks are dark with prickly hairs.

When the shop door finally closes, Mr Bao enters the back room.

"Doesn't it bother you to stand so close to a barbarian?" Mrs Yip asks.

"Why did you think that dead body was mine?"

Mrs Yip pounds her stick into the bubbling water. She swirls her stick and the shirts circle in its wake. A collar pokes up and Mrs Yip stabs. A sleeve flails above the current as if to grab hold of the tub's rim and thus escape.

"What do they do with the dead bodies?" she asks.

"Paupers are buried in mass graves."

"Where?"

Tonight, Mrs Yip walks to the outskirts of town. Crickets serenade her in the soft evening light. The ruins of the South

Station send shadowy fingers across the road but Mrs Yip's heart doesn't race. That is, not until she climbs the riverbank to gaze at the open pits below.

Inside the pits lie the bodies of the homeless, the poor and the unclaimed. Humans and dogs and cats alike. Or so Mrs Yip imagines. She can't bring herself to go any closer. She runs all the way back to Mr Bao's laundry.

As soon as he arrives the next morning, Mrs Yip asks, "Do you believe in an afterlife?"

"You've had some education, am I right?"

Mrs Yip nods. "The nuns told me that if I prayed to their god, I would go to a place called heaven where I could rest on clouds and listen to angels sing."

"I went to a missionary school, too. They told me the same thing. Do you believe that, Mrs Yip?"

"No."

"Neither do I."

"What about grave sweeping?" Mrs Yip asks.

"Do you mean those hungry ghosts who consume burnt food and wine? Who will haunt you if you don't clean their tombstone each spring? Folk tales and superstition! I believe in rational change. Expect great things from Chairman Mao."

* * *

Every morning, Mr Bao reads the *People's Daily*. By the time he finishes the newspaper, the pages hang limp. If he kept all those words to himself, Mrs Yip wouldn't mind. But Mr Bao must share it all while she washes and steams and starches.

Once Mr Bao finishes the day's reading, he invites Mrs Yip to share a pot of tea. Mrs Yip welcomes the break but knows what is coming. Every day, she tries to change the topic. She says, "All this talk of politics makes my head ache."

"What do you wish to discuss?" Mr Bao asks.

"Tell me why you joined the Party."

Mr Bao loves this question. He returns to it multiple times each day. But Mr Bao does not possess a storyteller's gift. He jumbles time and place. One day, he speaks of Shanghai. Another day, his attention resides in Hebei Province and with a missionary called Brother Ned. "He was an American," Mr Bao explains. "That's why I don't mind dealing with barbarians."

"What do missionaries have to do with the Communist Party?" Mrs Yip asks as she heats the flat irons. She's long ago grown bored of the question but it seems a small price to pay to avoid talk of politics.

Mr Bao's face darkens. Mrs Yip wonders if she's used too much firewood. But his ire is not directed at her.

"Brother Ned was one of the good ones. The others were not so kind. When my parents could no longer afford to pay my school fees, I was turned away. For years, I searched for a new spiritual home. I found the Communist Party."

When Mr Bao exhausts his store of childhood tales, he asks, "What about you, Mrs Yip?"

Mrs Yip's mouth is full of clothespins. She wrestles the stiff shirts off the clothesline and brings them inside to iron. Mr Bao lifts the load from her aching arms and piles the shirts on the counter. They protest and protrude like a graveyard of ghosts determined to rise.

"What about me?" she asks.

"What brought you to the Communist Party?"

"On the march from Shenzhen, the army commander said I could follow but I would only be fed if I joined the Party," she says.

Mr Bao can't imagine such a quid pro quo. He longs to practice what he preaches. He organises discussion groups for the workers in their alley. He sends Mrs Yip to recruit all her friends.

When no one appears, Mr Bao changes the focus to a reading session. "Not everyone can afford a copy of the *People's Daily*," he says. That effort also fails. Mr Bao casts about for some other way to spread the Communist message.

One morning, Mr Bao flings open the laundry's wooden door. He shouts, "Get up! Get dressed! We have work to do. I've decided that my business should belong to the people."

"You'll sell the laundry?" Mrs Yip asks. In her head, she calculates the profit Mr Bao will reap. She gazes at him with newfound admiration in her eyes.

"Of course, I won't sell. What a capitalist thought!" Mr Bao retorts. "Tonight, I'll leave the door unlocked so that the people can come inside and decide what to do."

"What about me?" Mrs Yip asks.

"You're one of the people. You can stay if you like."

Mr Bao writes posters in his finest calligraphy. He fully expects the people to continue the good work of a laundry. He leaves detailed instructions on how to operate the wringer and exactly how much soap to use.

Mrs Yip delivers the last load of shirts and pants. She returns to the laundry to find her friends from the alley already inside. She can hear their laughter through the open door and hurries to join the fun.

One of her friends climbs on top of the counter. He examines each of Mr Bao's posters.

"What do they say?" one of the workers asks.

"How would I know? I can't read," the man on the counter replies.

He removes a knife from his pocket and slashes the posters. The others cheer. They overturn buckets, tear the blue wrapping paper, and demolish the prized wringer.

Mrs Yip tries to stop them but they pin her into a corner and threaten her with her own stout stick. In the end, all she can do is grab her few possessions before her former friends chase her away with a broom.

* * *

Mrs Yip finds a new job as a trash picker. Every morning, she walks up Sinan Lu, her long prong at the ready. Every afternoon, she returns on Nanchang Road as her fork drags behind. She sleeps on the streets and eats what she finds. It's no life for an old woman like her but by now winter has come to Shanghai and it's too cold to walk all the way to Shenzhen.

Today is Mrs Yip's lucky day. She finds a whole daikon radish and stuffs it into the leg of her pants. Her mind searches for the recipes she once knew to cook such a root. Distracted, Mrs Yip swings her pitchfork. Mr Bao leaps out of the way.

"Mrs Yip! I've been looking for you everywhere."

"Why would you do that, Mr Bao?"

"I want to take you home with me."

Mrs Yip blushes.

"To my housing complex, that is. I've made arrangements for you to have a room. It's my fault you're out here on the streets. This is no place for a woman of your age."

His words knock the wind out of her.

"Do you have any belongings we should collect?" he asks.

Mrs Yip points to the horsehair blanket tied to her back.

Mr Bao leads the way. They stop at a stone archway. "Welcome to Peace Court," he says.

The entry is manned by a guard. Never mind that the man is asleep on the job. The alleys teem with street markets selling all a heart could desire: fruit, live fish, foot basins. Mrs Yip has never before lived in a place good enough for a shop owner.

In a sunny courtyard, Mr Bao points. "My wife and I live on the second floor of this building. Your new home is one floor higher. Go ahead. Take a look. The door is open."

Mrs Yip climbs the three flights of stairs. The steps are wooden and clean. Each landing has a water barrel and a stone shelf that serves as a cooking area. The hall smells faintly of millet.

At the top of the stairs, a door stands open and sunlight streams onto the landing. Mrs Yip cannot believe her luck. A whole room to herself with a big window. Below the window stands an empty cedar chest.

The chest is dented in one corner but if placed at the right angle and away from the light, it looks perfectly decent. Mrs Yip removes the horsehair blanket from her back. She transfers into that chest the possessions she's carried with her for so long: her wedding *qipao*,[3] the suit her husband was saving for special occasions and a pair of clogs her son once wore. She hangs the family portrait, taken at a seaside vacation long ago, on the wall, strategically positioned to hide a tear in the rose-patterned wallpaper.

Then the thought of so much luxury clutches at Mrs Yip's heart. Her husband would never approve. Mrs Yip hurries downstairs. Mr Bao waits in the courtyard as if he expected her.

"How much will this cost?" Mrs Yip asks. "How am I to pay? I don't belong in a place like Peace Court."

"I've paid your rent for the first three months," Mr Bao replies. "That should be enough time for you to find gainful employment."

"Why are you doing this for me?"

"I was wrong about the laundry. I deprived you of your income and a place to live. Please let me take responsibility and make amends."

Mrs Yip chews on his words. She casts her mind far and wide

3 A traditional Chinese form-fitting sheath dress, also known as a *cheongsam*.

from the brave Red soldiers to the pious nuns to the humble folk of Shenzhen. She can recall no example of such a magnanimous gesture.

Her eyes grow unaccountably moist. She turns her head to hide this unseemly emotion. The courtyard seems so sunny and clean. The sort of place where a boy like hers could grow up strong and free. A stone bench invites her to sit down and be at home.

"This isn't some kind of Communist experiment?" she asks.

"Absolutely not."

Mrs Yip sniffs. She plants herself on the bench. The stone warms her buttocks. "Well," she glares at Mr Bao. "Why don't you sit down, too?"

Author's Note

A story is like a shark. It can only swim forward.

This is a hard lesson for me to learn as I write. Most of my fiction is set in Shanghai, China, where my father was born. Many of my stories, like "Mrs Yip", exist within a historical context. I must convey that sense of time and place to my readers without boring them with a history lesson. In "Mrs. Yip", I have relied on details like the march to Peking or the banners in Shanghai to evoke a historic moment when power changed hands in China.

To create a character like Mrs Yip, I need to know her entire life story. Where she was born (Shenzhen), her favourite food (salted plums) and her deepest fear (an unmarked grave). I need to know how she and Mr Bao first met and what they thought of each other at that time. She probably found him a little silly at first.

I ask myself all these questions because Mrs Yip and Mr Bao both appear in my second novel, which I am writing at this moment. My problem is that my novel opens many years after Mrs Yip and Mr Bao first met. Both of them are also secondary characters to the central plot. It felt like their backstory was pushing my novel backwards in time rather than propelling it forwards like a shark. So, I cut out their backstory of how Mrs Yip came to live in Shanghai and how she met Mr Bao. The backstory remains important for me in order to write my novel but it's not necessary to share it with my readers. That would be like wearing all my clothes at the same time to show people I have them.

But as Mrs Yip's backstory lay on the cutting floor, it seemed to me that it writhed in pain. Here was a story that wanted to be told. Her backstory had life, humour and pathos. It was more than a list of biographical details. If her tale didn't fit the scope of my novel, I thought, perhaps it could live on as a standalone short story.

Of course, you can't just cut a section out of a novel and expect it to breathe on its own. I changed the narrator so that it's like a camera that sits on Mrs Yip's shoulder and sees the world more or less through her eyes. But the camera can also turn around and take a selfie. Like this – "See the rain pelt Mrs Yip's head as she kowtows in the mud."

A Tale of Three Grandmothers

Lalaine F Yanilla Aquino

The Philippines is a small country in Southeast Asia. It is an archipelago comprising more than 7,100 islands, of which three main islands are Luzon, Visayas and Mindanao. Its culture is unique. It is known to be a predominantly Christian nation in Asia; it is of Asia but not quite Asian in some regards. Its people are diverse in terms of culture, beliefs, temperament and socio-economic status, but they are some of the most hospitable, cheerful, resilient, welcoming, warm, patient, talented and hardworking people in the world.

A number of countries have colonised the Philippines: Spain for more than 300 years, the United States of America for more than 40 years and Japan for more than two years (during World War II). The influences of these colonisers can be seen in the Philippine languages (more than 150) and alphabet, in the country's cuisine and in the people's love for the arts. The people's names – their given names and family names – in themselves show the history of colonisation.

It is quite interesting growing up in the Philippines, particularly if you belong to a family whose elders belong to different ethnic groups in the country. You will grow up hearing the rhythm and music of various Philippine languages and being exposed to different (sometimes conflicting) beliefs about how to name one's children, how to pay respect to elders, and how girls and boys are expected to behave. It is strangely fun growing up as a youth in the Philippines.

Three grandmothers – that was what she had when she went to sleep last night. But just like that, when Luzvi woke up, she only had one left. She received the news with a surprisingly profound calmness she did not know she had. There was a little prick of pain in her heart, certainly. But she was calm.

It was *Nanay*[1] who told her about the death of Lola Liit[2] – her carefree, petite, *morena*[3] maternal great-grandmother who always had a naughty twinkle in her eyes. She had died peacefully in her sleep, in her cozy nipa hut in the small village of Mobo in Aklan Province.

It was *Tatay*[4] who told her about the death of Inanang[5] Estricia – her strict, regal, and *mestiza*[6] paternal grandmother who, after a lingering illness, died in her big mansion-like wooden house in the town of Tayabas in Quezon Province.

Two grandmothers – almost of the same age, both in their 80s – in two different island groups in the Philippines (in Luzon and Visayas) passing away at almost the same time, never meeting each other in their lifetime; yet their death seemed to wake Luzvi up from a dream, which was mostly happy but in some tiny parts confusing.

After telling Luzvi the sad news, her parents were in a bind. *Tatay* had to go home to Tayabas to pay his last respects to his mother. *Nanay* needed to go to Mobo with Lola Panching, Luzvi's maternal and only remaining grandmother, to pay their respects to Lola Liit. But what should they do with Luzvi and her four younger sisters?

While her parents were seriously discussing what to do, Luzvi slipped out of the bedroom. Theirs was a small place in the town of San Juan in the National Capital Region. It had a toilet, a small kitchen cum living room and dining room, and one bedroom, where all seven members of their family slept, in the first floor of a two-storey house, which had been divided into several rooms and

1 Mother in Tagalog.
2 Literally "little grandmother" in Tagalog.
3 Brown-skinned in Tagalog.
4 Father in Tagalog.
5 Grandmother in Tagalog.
6 A woman with mixed racial ancestry; in the context of the story, fair-skinned due to having Spanish blood.

rented out to different families. San Juan was about 436 kilometres away from Mobo, Kalibo, Aklan (one has to take a ship or a plane then a jeepney, a tricycle and a little banca boat across the Aklan river to get to Mobo from San Juan) and about 129 kilometres away from Tayabas, Quezon (one has to take a 30-minute jeepney ride, a four-hour bus ride, then a one-hour jeepney ride to get to Tayabas from San Juan).

Luzvi could still hear her parents talking when she went into the backyard, climbed up the *kamias* tree[7] and jumped onto the roof of the first floor. She got a ladder from its secret place on the roof (secret because only the caretaker should know where it was and used it only when doing repairs) and used it to climb to the roof of the second floor.

There in the middle of the roof, which provided her sanctuary when she wanted to have some time away from her noisy sisters or when she simply wanted to eat her favourite *pan de coco*[8] in peace, Luzvi sat and despite her sadness, she savoured the panoramic view. In the north was the old white church where her sisters were christened and where they usually lined up a day before Christmas to receive the gift from the parish priest (a bag of groceries, a few kilos of rice, and white shirts for the children). In the east were the palatial houses where showbiz personalities and politicians resided (that subdivision used to be a rice field across the stream which Luzvi and her friends would cross to pick *aratilis*[9] from the trees that grew abundantly around the rice paddies). In the south was her sisters' wooden haunted-house-like school which was actually a very large and old house which an enterprising Tsinoy had turned into a private elementary school. In the west, her elementary school surrounded with huge tamarind and star apple trees (she smiled to herself as she remembered how she used to climb those trees and was caught by no less than the school principal).

7 Bilimbi tree, a tall tree commonly found in backyards.
8 A popular bread roll or bun in the Philippines with sweet coconut filling.
9 The fruit from a kind of cherry tree found in the Philippines.

She thought she was enjoying the panoramic view, but warm tears flowed down her cheeks. She allowed herself to cry – for the tears to cleanse her heart.

* * *

She thought of Lola Liit – truth be told, she was Luzvi's favourite. When Luzvi was little and her great-grandmother was spending vacation with them, Lola Liit would always tickle her or measure Luzvi's height using her hand span. With Lola Liit, there was always something to laugh about. She would tell her stories: how Lolo Laki,[10] her husband, who was two full heads taller than she was, courted her.

"*May mas guwapo sa kanya*," (Another suitor was better looking than he was) she would tell Luzvi with that signature twinkle in her eyes, but she still chose the orphan from Iloilo. Lolo Laki was separated from his family during the Philippine revolution, the one where Filipinos fought against the Spanish colonisers. It was not clear to him if his parents had died during the war because he never saw them again and he was adopted by the family who took him to Aklan. Lolo Laki adopted the family name of his foster parents, but he still remembered the family name of his own family: Inovejas. Luzvi liked the sound of that name and she felt it fit Lolo Laki perfectly because compared to Lola Liit, he was very meek, he was a gentle giant.

What Luzvi found more fascinating was that Lola Liit did not know how to read and write. She had never gone to school. *I cannot imagine not being able to read and write!* But she was able to raise four children and manage the household with the meagre income of Lolo Laki, from serving as a porter in the wet market. Lola Liit also knew how to do a lot of things: she could make balls out of coconut leaves, sleeping mats out of *buri*[11] leaves and

10 Literally "big grandfather" in Tagalog.

11 A palm commonly found in the Philippines, the leaves of which are dried and woven into mats, bags, wallets, roofs, etc.

sweet *suman*[12] wrapped in fresh, young banana leaves. When she spent vacations with Luzvi's family, Lola Liit even "invented" a new dish using the scraps of meat left in the barbecue marinade that her parents usually just threw away after putting all larger pieces of pork tenderloin on sticks to grill and sell. Since then, the deliciously invented dish – the scraps of meat and the marinade – became a staple food for their family.

There was another thing Luzvi found fascinating about Lola Liit: she had never worn undergarments, neither bras nor panties. She would just wear her white chemise and her long overlapping skirt. So unlike Inanang Estricia, who always wore *a bestida* (a dress that reached below her knees), even when she was just at home.

Now that she came to think about it, Luzvi realised that not only was Inanang Estricia rather formal in the way she dressed, she was also rather formal when she was with her granddaughter. Luzvi never saw her smile. In the few times that she would talk to Luzvi when she was in Tayabas for the summer vacation, Inanang Estricia would just remind her not to run up and down the large wooden stairs, "*Baka ika'y magkabog diyan!*" (You might fall!) she would tell her, or tell her and her cousins not to bathe in the river under the old bridge past the lovely cathedral which had the longest aisle Luzvi had ever seen. *Would a groom grow impatient waiting for his bride at the end of that aisle?* Of course, when Inanang Estricia took her afternoon nap, Luzvi and her older cousins would slip out of the house, play and bathe in the river, and made sure they returned home before their grandmother woke up.

Luzvi thought of Inanang Estricia as a quiet presence in her life. She was like the mystic mountain of Banahaw that could be seen from the window of their house in Tayabas, silent but always

12 A Filipino delicacy, rice cakes made of glutinous rice cooked in coconut milk and often wrapped in banana or coconut leaves.

there. She quietly did her chores – mostly cooking the whole day – because she made sure that there was always food not only for everyone in the house, but for all visitors that came and went. Their home was like some kind of halfway house, there were always relatives, friends, or friends of friends stopping by, sometimes for a night or for a week. Luzvi did not know any of them, but they were always fed by Inanang Estricia and given a place to sleep in the house. Luzvi recalled how *Tatay* had explained to her the ways of Inanang Estricia.

"We used to be well-off, *Anak.*[13] Your Amamang[14] Jeremias was the best blacksmith in Tayabas. People from nearby towns would go to him to have their *karetela*[15] wheels and farm implements made."

Luzvi imagined the first floor of the huge wooden house which used to serve as Lolo Jeremias' *pandayan*[16] with all the workers who helped him. Inanang Estricia used to cook for all those workers, but during World War II, the Japanese seized their house and turned it into a garrison and they were only given a room where their family could stay. Since then, Lolo Jeremias' health gradually declined and he completely lost his workshop and his workers after the war.

"Was it losing the *pandayan* that made Amamang Jeremias and Inanang Estricia sad and sickly, *Tatay*?"

"It was not just that. They also lost five children during the war, to different kinds of illnesses. Only I, my Kuya Nonoy[17] and Ate Desa[18] were left."

Five children. Lost in a span of four years. That must have been the reason why Inanang Estricia always had that certain kind of sadness in her eyes. No parent ever got over losing a child. *Nanay*

13 Child in Tagalog.
14 "Amamang" is grandfather in Tagalog.
15 Horse-drawn carriage in Tagalog.
16 A blacksmith's workshop in Tagalog.
17 "Kuya" means older brother in Tagalog.
18 "Ate" means older sister in Tagalog.

had also lost a child twice: Luzvi's *kuya*, a baby boy lost when *Nanay* had a miscarriage months after she and *Tatay* got married, and the baby girl born after Luzvi who died from brain injury when she fell from the bed at the age of one. Every so often, *Nanay* would talk about those two babies, out of the blue, especially the baby boy who would have carried *Tatay*'s family name, Valencia.

When Luzvi was around six years old, Amamang Jeremias would often make her sit on his lap, hug her and tell her, "*Ito ang tunay na Valencia.*" (This is the real Valencia.) She did not know what to make of that, but when Amamang Jeremias passed away when Luzvi was eight years old, she remembered that and asked *Tatay* about it.

"You have cousins, but your grandfather did not think of them as Valencia because they are the children of Ate Desa, who now uses the family name of her husband," *Tatay* explained. Amamang Jeremias seemed content with Luzvi (and later her sisters) being a Valencia, but it was not the same for Inanang Estricia. "You should have a son," Luzvi heard her tell *Tatay*. And neighbours, mostly *Nanay's* friends, would often tease *Nanay*, "Surely you will have more than five children until you finally have a son." Perhaps that was the reason why it seemed more painful for *Nanay* to lose her baby boy.

"Lola Liit, should every family have a baby boy? What will happen if *Nanay* and *Tatay* do not have a baby boy?" Luzvi asked her great-grandmother once.

"That is nonsense! A baby boy is not a requirement. Every baby, girl or boy, is precious to God. Every baby is a gift. Your parents have been given five wonderful gifts already and I know that they are thankful," replied Lola Liit as she gave Luzvi a tight hug.

"What about using the family name? Are we going to lose the family name if there is no boy in the family?"

"You can always choose to use your own family name," Lola

Liit said firmly, looking into Luzvi's eyes. "You can choose to be anything and anyone you want to be," she continued.

"By the way, Lola Liit, why is my name different from those of my sisters? Why am I Luzvi and they are Irinea, Fidelisa, Celestina and Juliana?"

Lola Liit chuckled.

"That was a win for your mother!"

"A win?"

"Your sisters were named after saints found in the Roman Catholic calendar – they were named by your *inana*.[19] But you, my dear Luzvi, you were named by your mother. She had been to only two regions of the country: Luzon and Visayas. So you were named Luzvi."

That warmed Luzvi's heart. It made her name extra special. But she did not quite understand Lola Liit when she said that it was a win for *Nanay*. If she were to think of *Nanay* winning, it would be a win against Lola Panching. As far as Luzvi could remember, mother and daughter were always *contra pelo*.[20] And sometimes Luzvi was caught between them.

Lola Panching wanted Luzvi's hair in a ponytail. *Nanay* wanted Luzvi's hair untied.

Lola Panching insisted on Luzvi using a spoon and fork every time she ate. *Nanay* never discouraged Luzvi from using only her hands when eating with gusto.

Lola Panching taught Luzvi how to properly pick her teeth in public. There were no such lessons from *Nanay*.

Lola Panching wanted Luzvi to sit properly, with knees close together. *Nanay* did not have a say on how Luzvi sat as long as she was comfortable.

19 Grandmother in Tagalog.
20 Tagalog expression for taking the contrary or opposing view.

Lola Panching wanted Luzvi to wear more dresses. *Nanay* bought Luzvi more shirts and shorts.

Lola Panching wanted Luzvi to take afternoon classes, so she could help with chores in the morning. *Nanay* insisted that she stayed in her morning classes, and maintain her place in the top section of her batch and just study well.

Lola Panching did not want Luzvi to fight with anyone. *Nanay* taught Luzvi to defend herself when needed. And defend herself she did, not only herself but her sisters and friends as well.

There was a time when the son of their landlord pushed her youngest sister on the street. Luzvi saw this, helped her sister get up, and collared the culprit and told him he should not do that. Luzvi was only 11 years old at that time. The landlord summoned her to his living room, scolded Luzvi for collaring his son. Luzvi held back her tears and told the landlord what his son did to her sister. The landlord simply dismissed her and told her that her parents would certainly know about what she did. She was the first to report to her parents about what had happened, but this time, Luzvi was crying; she knew there was definitely something wrong about what the landlord did. What was it that she saw in her parents' eyes when she told them the story? Was it anger or hurt or helplessness, or a combination of these?

Sometimes she also saw that look in their eyes when Lola Panching scolded Luzvi's parents about certain decisions they made. Like when they transferred Luzvi's sisters to a private school after a public school teacher bullied Luzvi's youngest sister. *Nanay* insisted that she could not let her daughters stay in a school that would hurt them and make them unhappy. Luzvi had already graduated from the same public grade school at that time – she had experienced some kind of bullying from male classmates, some teachers and even from the school principal.

Luzvi never told her parents about these incidents: she fought when she could (she even had a fist fight with her male classmates when she defended her best friend from their bullying and she got hit in the stomach), explained her side when she knew what she did was right, accepted punishment when she knew she was at fault (like when she climbed the huge *sampalok* tree in the school yard or was caught bathing under the broken roof gutter of the library during class hours when the rain was pouring down).

Despite being called to the principal's office at least twice during her stay in that public school, Luzvi managed to graduate valedictorian. It was a proud moment for her dear parents and she was happy that they were happy. It was the least she could do for them. She wrote her own valedictory address. No one helped her. The teachers and guests were happily surprised that such insights and gratitude could be succinctly yet touchingly expressed by a 12-year-old.

Lola Panching was also there on her graduation day. She was proud and happy, too. She had always been supportive of Luzvi. When Luzvi was little and was assigned by *Nanay* to make their wooden floor shiny using a coconut husk, Lola Panching would secretly do the husking for Luzvi. Lola Panching also did not hesitate opening her piggy bank when Luzvi needed something for school: a costume for the field day demonstration, materials for a project in home economics or a novel for a literature class. Reading was one joy that Luzvi shared with her maternal grandmother – for someone who only reached the fourth grade, Lola Panching was a voracious reader. Lola Panching also did not hesitate to help Luzvi's parents, except that she would scold them first before she gave them what they needed. Aside from helping Luzvi's family, Lola Panching also helped her parents' and her brothers' families. One would think that Lola Panching was rich, but she was actually working as a *yaya*[21] for a middle class family

21 Tagalog word for one who works for a family to take care of the children.

and was barely earning the minimum wage. She was the eldest and only daughter in her family, and she did not even graduate from grade school. "But I was the smartest in my class – I could have been a teacher, if only we had the money to pay the two-peso tuition fee," Lola Panching had shared with Luzvi.

"If I were there, Lola Panching, I would have given you the two pesos from my piggy bank!" Luzvi replied. Lola Panching laughed and cried at the same time.

Luzvi's mother was Lola Panching's only child, born in Mobo in the last year of World War II, when they were frantically leaving their village because the Japanese soldiers were at their heels. Lola Panching was on a carabao cart[22] with the midwife, who helped her give birth to Luzvi's mother. Two years after Luzvi's mother was born, her father died of tuberculosis. Lola Panching never remarried though she was a widow at the age of 21. She left Aklan to find work in Manila and left her young daughter to the care of her mother. So Luzvi's mother grew up in the care of her grandmother, Lola Liit, and joined her mother in Manila only after she graduated from grade school. Lola Panching would sometimes complain that Lola Liit spoiled *Nanay,* and *Nanay* spoiled Luzvi and her sisters.

But Luzvi did not think so. *Nanay* made them work and disciplined them when necessary. Luzvi learned how to cook rice, clean milk bottles, wash the dishes and scrub the floor before she turned eight years old. Once, *Nanay* saw Luzvi throw a *tabo*[23] into their neighbour Aling Rosa's laundry basin to make the water splash from the basin and wet Aling Rosa's face. Luzvi had never seen *Nanay* so angry. That day, Luzvi learned the meaning of *respect.* Also, of *kindness.* Aling Rosa was a neighbour who always needed help, to buy medicine for her sick husband, to look for a teenage daughter who eloped, to help get a son out of jail, or

22 A cart pulled by a water buffalo.
23 A water dipper commonly used in Filipino homes as a cleaning and bathing implement.

simply to look for food to feed her five children. *Nanay* would always help her. Just because.

Maybe because her parents tried to give them enough that Luzvi did not really think their family was poor like Aling Rosa. *Tatay* was working as a messenger in a bank and *Nanay* was selling pork barbecue, *bananacue*,[24] *adobong mani*,[25] fishball and *haluhalo*[26] in front of their house. Luzvi would secretly pray that *Nanay* would not be able to sell all the *bananacues* because that was Luzvi's favourite and *Nanay* would always give her and her sisters what was left unsold. The first time Luzvi realised that they were rather poor was when Lola Panching's younger brother died of liver cancer, leaving eight young children behind.

"He wanted to eat *tinolang manok*.[27] I could not even cook that for him. I did not have the money," Lola Panching said, her voice trembling.

She did not have the money to cook *tinolang manok*. It was a simple dish. Luzvi thought it did not cost that much. Perhaps Lola Panching had no money anymore in her piggy bank. Perhaps she had not received her salary. Luzvi wanted to comfort Lola Panching, but she did not know how. There was more than grief at that moment. *Was it regret? Would Lola Panching also have regrets now that her own mother has died?* Perhaps not. She had tried her best to help her parents. She had always been a dutiful daughter though grumpy at times. Somehow, Luzvi knew that Lola Liit would not have regrets. She was one happy soul, always knowing how to work hard and play hard. She and *Nanay* were kindred spirits.

Would *Tatay* have regrets because he was not able to give

24 A Filipino snack of fried bananas with brown sugar sold on skewers.

25 A Filipino snack of fried peanuts with garlic.

26 A Filipino dessert made of crushed ice, evaporated or condensed milk, with various ingredients such as strips of young coconut, leche flan, sweet potato, saba banana, etc.

27 A traditional Filipino stew of chicken meat, green papaya or sayote, and moringa or malunggay, cooked with ginger and onions.

Inana a grandson? Was Inanang Estricia happy though she did not have a grandson? What do people think about most before they die? Did Inanang Estricia think of Luzvi and her sisters? Luzvi was certain that Lola Liit thought of them with a smile. Both Lola Liit and Inanang Estricia had lived their lives to the fullest, in their own little way, doing little big things for their family: cooking, sewing, mending, creating lovely things. Was that enough not to have regrets?

Would I be doing as my grandmothers did? Would I be a mother and a grandmother, too?

Somehow, that thought made Luzvi shiver a little. A mother. All her three grandmothers and even her own mother had their first child before they turned 19 years old. Luzvi was turning 19 in five years.

Uh oh. Nope.

Luzvi gazed at the sky. Up there on the roof, she seemed to be able to reach the cumulus clouds. This was one of her favourite things to do. Just looking at the sky. "Reading" the clouds and the stories they had to tell. The sky told her that there was so much that she could do. She could learn how to weave a mat using *buri* leaves, or cook several dishes and feed people non-stop, or help the likes of Aling Rosa just because, or make *tinolang manok* for her family, or invent names for her future children. More than that, she could write poetry and stories, she could teach little children how to read and write, she could win math competitions, she could become a world-class athlete, she could travel around the world or she could even become a rock star.

Luzvi was thinking of all the other things she could do as she climbed down from the roof and went back to their house. Her parents were waiting for her. It was *Nanay* who spoke first.

"Luzvi, we have only enough money for your *Tatay* to go to Tayabas and for me to go to Mobo. We cannot take any of you and your sisters with us. You have to take care of them while we are away."

I cannot even say goodbye to Lola Liit and Inanang Estricia.

But perhaps it was better that way. There was no need for goodbyes. She would remember them as they were. Or perhaps she would see them in her dreams.

Lola Liit, I will always be your Luzvi. Inanang Estricia, I will always be a Valencia.

Author's Note

I have always been fascinated by names, both given names and family names. I notice how some names tell a story, who gave them to whom, how they were "invented" and what meanings they hold for both the giver and the receiver. At the macro level, names also tell the story of a community, of a country. This fascination with names inspired me to work around this theme in relation to women's roles in a patriarchal society. And the best way to write about that theme is to tell the story of several generations of strong women who have influenced the life of a young woman. Such influence does not stop when the women die; in fact, such influence is made more pronounced upon their death, particularly in a patriarchal society.

The story I wrote is close to my heart because I grew up having three grandmothers (and a mother), all of whom were strong women who had triumphed over many challenges in life and managed to ironically and paradoxically meet and circumvent the expectations of a patriarchal society, despite their poverty and very limited resources and opportunities. I wanted to highlight the fact that their lives mattered and still matter. My story is a tribute to their indomitable spirit, to their love and passion for life and for their family.

I would like to believe that I continue the tradition of strength, steadfastness, resilience, and love and passion for life and family.

In my story, I have also tried to foreground how each woman, though as strong as the other, has a unique way of almost invisibly asserting herself, so that she could still live life on her own terms. I think it is a "skill" unique to women in a patriarchal society as to how to make others believe that they – the women – are actually "following the norms". And because they are all strong women, it is inevitable that they would "clash" at some point. Yet, such clashes are still healthy and productive as they can inspire the younger women to find their own strength.

Silence

Debasree Gosh

Balinese Hindus usher in the New Year in a unique manner. The celebrations begin with the annual event of *Melasti,* a purification ritual and ceremony where sacred implements are cleansed in the sea. This is followed by the *Ngrupuk* parade, where *ogoh-ogohs* which are effigies made of bamboo and styrofoam, are paraded and burnt to purify society. Subsequently, the Balinese observe *Nyepi*, a day of absolute silence and introspection. The day after *Nyepi*, the people participate in the *Dharma Shanti* procession to pray for forgiveness, peace and love within the community. Each ritual is intricate and deeply symbolic.

"We can never have too many flowers, Ni-Wayan," my grandmother said, as she looked over my shoulder at our local flower seller, Nyoman's wares. "Pick up some more of the white *cempaka*."[1] I bent over the majestic colours of floral blooms and sprays, woven like an enchanted carpet and watched Nyoman sprinkle some water over them to keep their freshness. *Dadong*[2] was holding a traditional offering of a *canang sari*,[3] spilling over with dark green betel leaves and vivid flowers, to take to our local *pura*.[4] Despite my 15 years, I felt a child-like thrill and magnificent excitement trickle down my spine.

With our hands full of offerings, we began our brisk walk to our local temple, from where the *Melasti* procession was slated to begin. The sun and clouds played hide-and-seek, and a light breeze, redolent with festive anticipation, played with our hair.

1 A fragrant flower from a large evergreen tree.

2 Grandmother in Balinese.

3 A small, delicately folded palm-leaf basket carrying offerings to the god Sang Hyang Widhi Wasa.

4 A Balinese temple.

The *pura segara*[5] was bustling with worshippers as the sea roared all around us, a grand old sight with its snow-capped waves. We entered through the garden of the *jaba pisan*,[6] which connected the bustling world outside to the spiritual centre within. Next, we walked into the *jaba tengah*,[7] where our beloved elderly *gamelan*[8] musician was playing on his *bonang*[9] in the music pavilion. We walked past the *bale kulkul*[10] and entered the sacred heart of our temple, the *jero*,[11] where our most sacred relics were kept.

Balinese Hindus believe in the Supreme God of Sang Hyang Widhi Wasa, also known as Acintya. I always looked up in awe at the *padmasana,* an empty throne in honour of the formidable, formless God. Most importantly, our temple was renowned for its possession of two holy ancient masks of the patron spirits Barong and Rangda. Barong was the spirit which protected our villages and Rangda symbolised the feminine energy of the Goddess Durga.[12] On *Melasti,* the idols of the gods and other sacred implements, including the famous masks, were taken to the sea for an ablution, a ritual held a few days before *Nyepi.* As a child, I wondered why they only bathed once a year, when I was scrubbed down with handmade coconut soap every day. As the ceremonial procession began, a beautiful sound wafted through the temple compound, as Ketut's nimble fingers graced the *bonang.* I joined the colourful group of worshippers, as we walked to the beckoning sea.

My name is Ni-Wayan and I live with my grandmother in a little house in the village of Banjar Kaja Sesetan in Denpasar, Bali, where I attend school. *Dadong* and I moved here a decade

5 A temple by the sea.
6 The outer zone of a Balinese temple.
7 The middle zone of a Balinese temple.
8 A traditional Indonesian music ensemble of bronze instruments.
9 One of the instruments in a gamelan ensemble.
10 A pavilion or tower-like structure which houses a slit-log drum in a Balinese temple.
11 The most sacred and holy zone of a Balinese temple.
12 An important deity in Hinduism, a goddess known for fighting evil.

ago from our ancestral village when I was five. To this day, I'm in the dark about why we moved at all. We hardly ever spoke of my mother and my memories of her remain in the vague folds of yesterday. My lasting memory of her is of a strong scent of lemon on her fingers, on a day long ago when I turned four in our old village. *Ibu*[13] and I were plucking lemons from our backyard and squeezing them into little wooden tumblers. Round-eyed, I watched my mother's beautiful, tired face glittering in the waning sun, as she smiled into my eyes. I felt an inexplicable diffidence around her, and somehow, comfortably uncomfortable, possibly because I saw so little of her. "N-I-W-A-Y-A-N," she spelt out, "my seven defining letters," she said, as she gathered me onto her lap. "*Ibu* misses you and works for you, and the day will come when we will always be together."

"When?" I asked, my eyes still wide from the shock of the sour lemon I had squeezed into my mouth.

"Soon," she said.

"Why do you always go away?" I would ask, as she hugged me goodbye each time before she left. "Wait for me," she'd say.

"You're as strong as Durga, *Ibu*," I said on the last day I saw her. I must have been seven.

She stood at the door, her graying hair loose, and her hands trembling from our lingering hug. She smiled in surprise and quickly turned and passed through the door. *Ibu* had been reading the story of Goddess Durga to me every night from an illustrated book she had brought with her, and the goddess's ten hands and acts of bravery enthralled me. But to my four-year-old self, Durga was also a mother, tender, fumbling, vulnerable, loving. Even mothers needed to be loved and encouraged. I hardly witnessed a conversation between *Dadong* and *Ibu*.

13 Mother in Indonesian.

And then she stopped coming. *Dadong* never spoke of her, and there was a tacit understanding that I wouldn't either. I didn't even have a phone number to call or an address to write a letter. I'd never seen my father, though I yearned to know of him. "He's dead," was *Dadong*'s repeated curt reply to my questions about him.

Once, when I was 13, I had dared to broach the subject at our simple dinner table. *Dadong*'s quiet reticence always frightened me, but I mustered the courage to bring up my mother.

"*Dadong*, did you make mother go away? Did you not like her?"

Silence and a stony yet surprised glance from her dark eyes met mine. I had hoped she'd get angry and erupt like Mount Agung, but she continued eating her *lawar*,[14] in her placid manner.

I tried again. "Why don't you tell me about *Bape*?[15] Did you think he was bad? I read a story in school in which there were no villains or heroes, and everyone was just an 'in-between'. Maybe my father was an 'in-between', maybe he was misunderstood?"

My ears caught the sound of steady chewing, broken only when my grandmother stopped to take a sip of *kopi luwak*,[16] an occasional indulgence she treated herself to.

Frustrated, I stood up and threw my spoon down on the table, my eyes filled with hot tears. I picked up our old salt cellar, and in a fit of uncharacteristic rage, emptied it in my dinner bowl and stormed out. The next morning, I didn't even dare to apologise, muted by my grandmother's stony silence as well.

After that, I stopped asking altogether. I was still too young to grasp the adult complexities of life. My little soul absorbed *Dadong*'s feelings and views like a sponge, with no resistance and rejection. The ache grew in my heart with each passing year, as I sifted through the cobwebs of age and time.

14 A dish of minced meat, coconut, spices and vegetables.

15 Father in Balinese.

16 Coffee produced from the partially digested coffee cherries consumed and defecated by the Asian palm civet.

As I immersed myself in the beautiful *Melasti* procession, my grandmother wafted into the crowd, to offer her flowers to the sea.

Suddenly, a loud noise broke my turbulent tryst with the past, and jerked me back to the present. "*Durga, Durga!*" I could hear a chant go up in the air, as the voices rose and fell, as though competing with the crash of the waves and the resounding music of the *gamelan*. Chaos seemed to have broken out amidst the din and commotion of the procession. Ni-Made, my school friend, saw me and ran up to me.

"The ancient Rangda mask, bearing holy inscriptions, is missing! It has been in our temple for so many years!" she panted.

I ran ahead and saw the head priest sitting with his head in his hands, and I noticed how helpless and dejected he looked. "What a sin, what an impure act!" he was shouting.

"Did the sea carry it away?" an old lady asked.

"No," the priest wailed as he shook his head. "No, no, I had just placed the idol on the sand and was washing the Holy Bell, and I was so preoccupied." He always entered a trance-like state during the cleansing of holy objects.

"How was I to know that we have a thief in our midst? The sea does not steal, it only cleanses."

The wind had started blowing wildly, in keeping with the mood of the people. Most of the worshippers had put their hands in the air, and a few younger priests started hunting around among the crowds. I looked around for my grandmother, but couldn't spot her in the disorder. No one seemed to know where the mask of Rangda had gone, and no one reported seeing anything suspicious. The air was permeated with a tense silence, as suspicion descended on each of our shoulders, shaking our impure souls.

"Rangda's infinite power cannot be captured in a mask or confined to it," I told Ni-Made as we trudged home. The festive atmosphere of this special day had been dampened beyond repair.

With the imminent approach of *Nyepi,* the Day of Silence, the town had been gearing up for our special way to commemorate the new year. I never found *Nyepi* to be particularly challenging. It was a day to observe restraint, quiet and abstinence, when one could articulate only through silence. My life with *Dadong* was an extension of *Nyepi,* the only exception being the moments when we ate our meals. Ni-Made shook her head: "Even so, that mask is almost 600 years old, and is sacred beyond thought, and as old as the oldest trees of Denpasar. It cannot be lost. It's like losing the very soul of our village."

I nodded and we parted as I slipped into our home. I felt the loss keenly myself. In the absence of my mother, I visited our temple every morning before school, to absorb the energy of Rangda. I even dared to imagine her fierce eyes penetrating my heart like a loving laser, illuminating my emptiness with hope, strength and compassion.

"Did you hear about the mask of Rangda, *Dadong*?" I shouted as I saw her pottering around the kitchen stove, frying some peanuts.

"Have a bite to eat, and then help me dry the clothes," she said.

Amazed at her composure, I said, "*Dadong*, where were you? The head priest is very upset. The mask has been stolen. Surely you are concerned?"

"Can God ever be stolen?" she replied in her cryptic manner. "I'm sure it will return to the temple very soon."

I felt aghast. *Dadong*, who followed rituals like a schoolgirl with her timetable, seemed nonchalant and apathetic.

"Then, does God have to be cleansed? Why do we need to purify her mask, when it's we who are so horrible?" I shot back with uncharacteristic teenage angst, as I sat down at the kitchen table.

"Because she absorbs all our mud," she said and turned away.

The very next day, whispers went around our village that the

Ngrupuk parade would go on as planned, on the eve of *Nyepi*. During this parade, our village's inhabitants would dress in their festive best and throng the roads to watch the procession of the big, bad *ogoh-ogohs,* the effigies of monsters. The village youth paraded them around on flat planks made of bamboo and timber, rotating them counter-clockwise three times at junctures. These effigies met their fates in the depths of the many bonfires which blazed across the village at the end of the parade, as they represented evil. As a child, I had been very scared of them, of their enormity of scale and abject features.

The previous year, we had a controversial *ogoh-ogoh* in the form of a figure dressed in shocking pink, who was holding a selfie stick, as a critique of the narcissistic exhibitionism catalysed by social media. Some of the crowd had cheered, while others roared in displeasure claiming that the selfie stick was a symbol of empowerment. The debate was resolved when it was unanimously decided not to burn the effigy but to donate it to an art museum in Ubud. *Ogoh-ogohs* represent *Bhuta-Khala*, the relentless forces of eternal time and energy. This year, however, the mood was sombre. This year, the musicians played a grim tune, and a group of people had put together a quick effigy of a figure who had both hands behind his back, as though hiding something not rightfully his, akin to the robber of Rangda's mask. It was burnt with great gusto at our crematorium, and everyone overtly and covertly expressed the same sentiment – that the mask of Rangda should be returned to the *pura* to reside with Barong's mask.

That night, *Dadong* and I walked home, in silent exhaustion. *Dadong* earned the small income we lived on by selling jars of her famous *sambal matah*[17] to three local cafeterias. She had worked as a cook in various restaurants until she turned 70, and her frugal

17 A Balinese raw spicy condiment similar to a salsa, made of chillies, shallots, garlic, lime and other ingredients.

ways ensured that we had enough to get by on. "I hope you go on to use your education well, maybe you can be a teacher," she would often suggest, when she saw me bent over my books. At 15, I knew that my grandmother would have to slow down sooner rather than later.

My grandmother never ate or drank water on *Nyepi*. We would arise at 5am and she would take a long drink of water and we would sit down to a simple breakfast of cooked black rice with coconut milk. We ate a banana each. *Dadong* did not encourage me to fast. She would cook a simple meal after we returned from the *Ngrupuk* parade and ask me to eat it through the day. "Drink plenty of water, too," she would caution, as I tended to get dehydrated.

As the first rays of the early sun ushered in *Nyepi*, my grandmother and I stirred in our bed. We slept together on a large double bed. Despite her few words, her presence comforted me and I drew sustenance from her quiet breathing. We sat down for our morning meal at the break of dawn, which was to be *Dadong*'s only meal until 6am the following day. I noticed how sad and shaken she looked, rather different from her poised and reserved self. I washed up the bowls and we went into the living room, treading softly and cautiously, silence clinging to my body like a garment. It was our day of introspection, where we journeyed within. I looked out of the window and saw a small group of *pecalang*[18] dressed in their checked black and white *sarongs*,[19] white shirts and black waistcoats, with a small dagger attached to the back of their headbands.

I cannot articulate what I felt when I turned back from the window and looked back into our living room. *Dadong* was sitting on our wooden floor, her eyes closed, tears streaming in little rivulets down her wrinkled cheeks. The ancient mask of

18 Local Balinese security officers.

19 A garment made up of a long length of fabric worn wrapped around the waist by both men and women.

Rangda had been lovingly placed on her red sacred cloth, spread on a small plank in front of her. Shock waves coursed down my spine, and I felt nausea and nervousness pulling me down to the floor. My grandmother – impeccable, upright and respectful – was a thief! How could she have stolen the sacred mask of Rangda, which had reposed in the inner chamber of the *pura* for generations? How could she have done this during the *Melasti* ritual, a time for cleansing our sins and not committing new ones? The sea was her witness, I thought, as tears kept running down her cheeks while her eyes remained closed. She was a brisk walker, and I imagined how she must have deftly wrapped it in her cloth, which had been tucked into her outfit, and quickly and deceitfully drifted away, her slight frame engulfed in the crowds and music.

Dadong stayed in the same position the entire day, as I practised deep breathing to calm my furious mind. *Nyepi* was a day of calm repose, and though every cell of my body was badly shaken, I couldn't defeat the purpose of our sacred day, loaded with lineage and legacy. Did she want to pray exclusively to Rangda? But did God not hear every muffled prayer?

I realised that day how we often, consciously or subconsciously, placed our elders on pedestals which occupied the highest peaks of our respect. Although tough situations stretched our reverence like elastic, we never want it to snap. Is this why we felt particularly bad whenever we were let down by our parents? I had often felt let down by mine, but continued to justify their actions as I wrangled with my emotions on my midnight pillow.

The minutes melted into hours like hot, molten wax slithering down the sides of a spent candle. I sat by the window and cast a fishing net around my thoughts to gather them in. Afternoon was paving the path for evening to descend, and a still silence pervaded our jolly little lane, which on other days resonated with laughter, vehicles and footfalls. Every Balinese had gone within the recesses of their minds, to part the curtains of their consciousness, to return to that primal, secret zone, which remained impervious to others. Eternal memories resurfaced on the shore of my mind, of my mother, whose hair was grey before her time, of her thin hands and faraway eyes, the tip of her beautiful nose just within reach of memory, but beyond the ambit of my reality. My father's quiet absence allowed me to shape his character in any way I wished, as I had never seen him in person or even in a photograph. The reality of parenthood was a fantasy for me.

When night painted the sky with its inky brush and dotted it with twinkling stars, I saw *Dadong* still sitting in front of the mask. We never put any lights on during *Nyepi*, but in the darkness I saw that there were no more tears streaming down her cheeks. Her breathing was hoarse and heavy. She seldom sat on the floor owing to a persistent ache in her lower back, which she had obviously disregarded today. The Rangda mask, with its matted hair and long tusks looked steadily back at her, and the two seemed to be communicating in a manner which was completely beyond my comprehension.

I kept a silent vigil with my grandmother all night. As the sun rays flooded our room, I saw my grandmother lovingly wrapping the mask of Rangda in her sacred cloth, and sprinkling holy water on it from a little jar. She was muttering something and I think I caught the word "forgiveness". The next minute, she turned and walked towards the door without a word. Her legs and back must have been aching as she was limping and wincing as she took her steps. Concerned, I ran after her, but a quiet pleading in her eyes stopped me as she stepped outside.

After some time, *Dadong* walked back in, empty-handed. She looked frail and fragile. "Have some water," I offered, as she sat down at the table to quench her thirst. I began peeling a banana for her. She accepted the fruit with trembling fingers and ate quickly, giving into the very human need of hunger. She then looked at me and said, "Get ready for *Ngembak Geni*,"[20] a ceremony for relighting the fire at the *pura* the morning after *Nyepi*, and handed me a small red envelope with my name on it. It wasn't sealed and my fingers fumbled as I took out a letter. "Read it upstairs," *Dadong* said weakly, and I tore up the stairs.

It was a handwritten letter, on neatly stapled pieces of foolscap paper.

My dearest Ni-Wayan,

I've loved you and kept you near me every minute of my life. There are some unspoken things which linger between present and past.

Let me tell you my story. You must have often watched the Omed-omedan[21] *ceremony which is celebrated in our village. The one in which boys kiss girls the day after* Nyepi *to commemorate love and a new beginning. I participated for the first time when I was 20. I had heard of the union of many couples through this ceremony, but I was never a confident girl. I felt that no one would approach me, let alone kiss me, plain as I was, but I went all the same that year.*

As the festivities began, I stood in a corner while my friends eased into the fun much more easily. After several minutes, I caught sight of a young man smiling at me. He was standing in the distance, and seemed to be observing the festival without participating in it. A flash of joyous recollection coursed through me. I knew him. Your dadong and his mother used to work together at a small food stall years ago. As children, we were taken to their workplace and made to sit on a wooden bench outdoors while they cooked in the kitchen. We would

20 A ceremony held the day after *Nyepi*, which include traditional rituals and social activities.

21 Known as the "Kissing Ritual", an annual ceremony held after *Nyepi* by the young people in Banjar Kaja Sesetan in Denpasar, Bali.

always play together and he was very kind to me. He never teased or ignored me like the other boys in school. He would hold my hand and we would run around happily. We looked forward to our little play dates amidst the aromas of the kitchen. Once work finished, our mothers would bring out some noodles and chicken, which we would all relish. Sometimes he would take some of his food and heap it onto mine, just to share.

But everything changed one day. We were playing with a blue kite when we suddenly heard a heated exchange between our mothers. Our mothers had often taught us not to fight and so we laughed in surprise on hearing their raised voices. Suddenly, they emerged from the kitchen. I felt myself being pulled away and his mother secured him on her lap. The kite tore, each of us clutching a piece. As our mothers walked away from each other, I wondered what they had fought over. An extra spice? A burnt utensil? We never knew. We never crossed paths nor saw them again in our little village.

And here he was, after so many years, at the Omed-omedan *ceremony. That little boy now chiselled into a man of 23. Despite the lapse of years, neither of us had any difficulty recognising one another. Embarrassed, I averted my gaze, but he came up and planted a slow kiss on my cheeks. Suddenly, I felt buckets of water drenching us. I clumsily slipped and fell, but he picked me up and put me back on my feet. "Will you marry me? I've thought of you every day, and hoped we'd meet again," he whispered through our tears.*

You must think of me as being very silly, but I always believed that love struck us in a moment, like a flash of lightning, and then gradually dissolved into our beings with the passing years. Magnificently happy and wet, we walked home together and your dadong *answered the door. Sharp as she was, she recognised him at once, and the significance of us returning hand in hand from the ceremony dawned on her. We exchanged formal pleasantries and he said: "We moved to Jakarta with my father eight years ago. My mother has asked me to pass on her regards."*

"May we have your blessings to marry?" he asked your dadong.

I'd hoped she would wrap him in an embrace but all she said was, "If that's what you have decided, that's what you shall do." With that, she walked out of the room.

I pleaded with her to be happy for us. Did she really bear a grudge over some long-forgotten fight with his mother? "It's your life," was all she would say.

"Ibu, will you come with us to Jakarta?" I asked. "I'll never leave Bali," she said.

Following a low-key marriage with a silent dadong, *we proceeded to Jakarta. My mother-in-law seemed eager to start afresh and was kind to me.* Dadong *was never rude to my in-laws but remained aloof. I was, however, very happy in Jakarta. On our first wedding anniversary, you were born, and your father gifted me the torn blue kite he'd treasured for years. We came back to Bali for a fortnight with you, and your* dadong *was happy to bless you. In Jakarta, we were successfully running a family food stall together. Oh, what a cruel twist of fate that your beloved father succumbed to a sudden illness when you were just three. I had lost my father, your grandfather, when I was five. It was horrible. Both his parents died within a year of him, and I was devastated.*

I had you to raise and the restaurant to run. I immediately came back to Bali and requested your dadong *to come to Jakarta to help me.* Dadong *was adamant that you stayed with her and asked me to focus on the business in Jakarta. Perhaps she loved me too much to forgive me – she'd brought me up with lots of expectations. I should have fought harder to keep you with me, but I was frightened of disobeying her again. She insisted that you were happy in Bali and I harboured the hope that one day I would be successful enough to reunite with you.*

And now, I'm about to slip away, dear putri[22] *… I've been very ill. I've battled this disease for many years now, and you wouldn't know me if you saw me. I didn't tell your dadong about my cancer because I felt that even my disease would disappoint her. Your dadong is a strong woman, please be kind to her. She has brought you up so well.*

I love you,
Your Ibu

I had read that we shed our cells as we touched things, and I held the letter to my face, hoping my mother's cells would merge with mine, and create meaning through some form of inert, immeasurable interaction.

As *Dadong* and I walked towards the temple for the *Ngembak Geni* ceremony, she said: "I have returned the mask of Rangda. I have sinned beyond measure and I took it to ask for forgiveness. I received your mother's letter last week. I read it, too. My prejudices and rigidity have hurt my daughter. I deserve no better, but you do. No penance is good enough. Rangda could be cleansed of my sins only through the *Melasti* of my tears." Her eyes were alight with pain and remorse.

I looked sideways at her profile, at how hunched she looked, burdened by her years of wrath, prejudice and recalcitrance. She had aged a decade in a week.

As we stood in the swirl of sweet-smelling incense and were enveloped by the steady rhythm of the *kendang*,[23] I felt a strange sense of calm which accompanies manic grief, a calmness which ensures we keep breathing although we feel like suffocating.

The temple elder came around to us when the *Dharma Shanti* procession began, and my grandmother fell at his feet.

22 Daughter in Indonesian.
23 A traditional drum, one of the instruments in a gamelan ensemble.

"Please, please, stand up, you have told me all. Sometimes confession is the best form of cleansing. What happened will remain between us," he said.

Worshippers greeted one another asking for forgiveness, as was the custom, and told the miraculous story of how the mask of Rangda had returned to the sacred interior of the temple. I marvelled at how beautiful our cultural heritage was, how age-old practices helped us, eventually, to become more complete human beings. Yes, that's what we were: flawed, repentant, passionate and compassionate humans, nothing less and nothing more.

"Can you forgive me, Ni-Wayan?" *Dadong* whispered, clasping my palm as we trailed along with the *Dharma Shanti* procession.

Author's Note

This story emerged from the very personal space of losing my grandmother this year. I was very close to her and it was cathartic to explore the relationship between Ni-Wayan and her grandmother, so writing this story was an intimate and complex experience. Although it is not autobiographical, I have infused elements of love reserved between a grandmother and her granddaughter.

I wished to explore how cultural heritage shapes one's personal beliefs and contributes to individual narratives. This involved deep research as I wanted to be true to the representation of Balinese culture and beliefs, and weave a creative story around the cultural context.

I consciously situated the story in the midst of the Balinese New Year celebrations and included the key rituals and festivals, such as *Melasti*, the *Ngrupuk* parade, *Nyepi* and the *Dharma Shanti* procession. "Silence" developed in tandem with my research on Balinese culture. Ni-Wayan's perspective gives us glimpses into the life she's had, the life she yearns for and the life she will leave behind.

Nyepi, the Balinese Day of Silence, allows the protagonist to engage in deep introspection, and this is central to the story, but what I wished to focus on was how learning and introspection can occur at any age, reflected in the growth of the grandmother in her twilight years.

If I were to summarise the story in one word, I would probably use the word "reflection" – on ourselves, on our relationships and on our surroundings. The use of Balinese words is meant to infuse the story with an indigenous flavour.

I've aimed to show how subjectivities permeate the narrative and create layers of life by using the first-person narrative voice.

Si Larut

Ismim Putera

Elephants were an important mode of transportation for the monarchy and elite in Malaya (now Malaysia). Besides having them work in plantations, elephants were often involved in important ceremonial celebrations such as the coronation of a Malay king. Elephants were regarded as royal animals and some were further trained to be war elephants. By the mid-19th century, tin ore mining flourished and became a major trade in some Malay states. The elephants were extremely useful for clearing new land for mining sites.

It was noted that Malay animal trainers were very skilful in talking to elephants. They shouted out certain phrases which instructed the elephants to do very specific tasks. In the Malay society, this skill was highly valued for its practicality, and thus learning them was essential. The trainers were also very knowledgeable in taking care of sick or wounded elephants using herbal plants. This unique human-animal interaction was documented in books written by many British colonial administrators who called it the "elephant language".

One day, an elephant that was being used by the miners escaped into the adjacent jungle. When recaptured it was found to be covered with mud rich with tin.

– Khoo Kay Kim, *Taiping (Larut): The Early History of a Mining Settlement*

A flash of betel nut red – blood in his eyes.

Long Zahir wipes it away with his sleeve. In the heat of combat, his vision doubles under the rays of the late afternoon sun. Sweat from his brow streams onto his cheeks, dampening his dimples. He blinks multiple times to clear his vision.

Two weeks ago, Si Larut, the royal elephant, had escaped from its pen in Istana[1] Meranti. The unhappy king had decreed that it should be retrieved by any means.

Now, Long Zahir and his men are confronting a herd of angry wild elephants on a grassy plain near Mount Korbu. Si Larut is presumed to be hiding somewhere amongst the bamboo groves stretching all the way to the jungle fringes.

He wipes the remaining smudge with his fingers to get another sharp look at the miracle before him. Another wild elephant is down. A spear had pierced its right leg. He turns his face away from the gruesome wound. The unnecessary killing of these animals is, indeed, a fruitless exercise. The rest of the wild elephants, about 50 of them, have fearfully retreated back into the bamboo groves flourishing at the foot of Mount Korbu.

"*Hoh-hoh*!" shouts Long Zahir. It means "stop" in elephant language. Senduduk, his pet elephant, lifts her trunk skyward and trumpets loudly to signal the other elephants to stop marching forward.

"We did it, *Tuan*![2] We've chased them off!" A man shouts loud and clear from afar. The soldiers join in the cry of triumph. They flag their spears with pennants high while others use them as crutches to keep standing upright. They pant slow and heavy, and bleed and swelter in their rattan armour suits.

"Long Zahir, they've become too wild. I wish we can stop killing these poor creatures," mentions Kitang, a senior minister working in Istana Meranti. Apart from being an expert in talking to elephants, he settles taxation and advises Long Jaafar, the King, on matters pertaining to British administration. For the past four days, he has been assisting Long Zahir to devise attack and defence formations using trained elephants. He is at his wits' end trying to win the battle against those wild elephants. Deep in the recesses

1 An istana is a royal palace.
2 "Sir" or "Lord" in Malay, a respectful form of address.

of his mind, he believes a penumbra of mischievous *hantu hutan*[3] might be interfering with their pursuit.

"I agree, Kitang." Long Zahir blinks rapidly for a few moments. "Those wild elephants are not to be taken lightly. *Hantu hutan* must have made them very violent. I hope Si Larut can protect himself."

> **They are known as Hantu Hutan – the Spirits of the Forest – and are as real to the Malays and as much dreaded as the tigers and other wild animals of the forest.**
>
> – **Sir George Maxwell**, *In Malay Forest.*

Rembulan waves at Long Zahir. He is a Siamese slave working in Istana Meranti. He runs forward and assists his master to get down from Senduduk's back.

"*Tuan*, you're injured. You must lie down!"

"Bring him back to the tent. I'll help him defend this place," orders Kitang sternly. His voice quivers for a moment. He is standing a stone's throw away from the dying elephant. He can sense the aura of a restless *hantu hutan* crawling out from the circular wound, mocking him. A few moments later, the poor elephant lets out a sickening snort before it is overtaken by complete stillness.

Kitang's lips are as white as polished limestone. His suntanned face is as rough as stone slabs. A sudden gust of wind blows dust over his left cheek.

"It's dead," mumbles a young soldier while closing the elephant's pearly eyes. He covers the carcass with alternating layers of coconut and banana leaves.

"They'll be back," confirms Kitang, straining a smile but his teeth are maroon red, stained by years of chewing young areca

3 Literally means "ghost of the forest" in Malay, also refers to spirits residing in the forest.

nuts. "I can smell their fear and anger from here. They're hiding behind those bamboo trees. I know Si Larut is there, too."

* * *

Long Zahir rests on a *mengkuang* mat,[4] panting fast. The tent is scorched by heated afternoon air. Rembulan pours clean water into a coconut shell bowl.

"*Tuan*, drink this. Your body is burning hot."

"Thanks." Long Zahir finishes the water in one gulp. He then lies back on the mat, continuing to groan.

Kitang elbows his way into the tent and eyes Long Zahir with disapproval. "You broke the formation, Long Zahir. That wild elephant could have easily pushed you down from Senduduk's back. If you had slipped and fallen, you could have been squashed under their feet. Luckily your men distracted the elephants and detoured them towards the bamboo grove."

Long Zahir's wide grin falters as he looks at Kitang, whom he regards as his uncle since his adolescent years. It was Kitang who had taught him *silat*,[5] and, of course, to ride elephants.

"It works, right?"

Kitang stretches his lips into a hard line. "You could've been hurt, *Tuan*, that's all. What am I supposed to tell the King later? Those are not the usual ones that feed on sugar canes."

Long Zahir closes his eyes and sees swirling red and yellow lights. He replays the events over and over in his mind. He may have won the battle against the wild elephants today, but may not tomorrow. He expected the King to deploy more strong men today but, sadly, none of them have showed up to assist him.

"I didn't expect catching Si Larut to be this hard." Long Zahir formulates his thoughts. He has many tactics up his sleeve but none had really worked against those burly animals.

4 A mat made of screw pine leaves.

5 A collective term for a class of indigenous martial arts from the Nusantara and surrounding areas of Southeast Asia.

The elephants are not some lowly animals. They once lived in Kayangan, a mystical kingdom in high heaven. They were sent down to the earth by the gods themselves.

Long Zahir sits up and takes off his shirt.

"How's everyone?"

"I've instructed them to build tents and light up bonfires. The river is just behind the bush, not far from here." Kitang throws some herbal leaves into a ceramic bowl and grinds it with a wooden pestle.

"Rembulan, put this on your master's chest and back."

Rembulan dabs the poultice onto his red skin. A dark green liquid oozes out and stains the edge of the wound. Long Zahir hisses slowly, as if scraping off a stubborn leech clinging on his chest.

"We've done well this time, but …" Long Zahir admits his flaw, "I should not have changed the formation. That was entirely my fault."

"Si Larut is somewhere near. I can hear his heavy footsteps." Kitang assures him. "Sleep early tonight. We begin tomorrow morning. Our men deserve good food and rest tonight."

By sunset, steam and spices fill the air as bowls of *nasi himpit*[6] are served all around for supper. Long Zahir sprinkles powdered nipa palm sugar into his coconut shell bowl. Misty steam coils around his fingers.

Enough blood has been shed today, from both men and animals, and thinking about it gives Long Zahir bouts of intense headache. Pain like the sting of a thousand centipedes is gnawing at his lower back. Once the sweetened rice satiates his hunger, he looks up only to find Rembulan and Kitang missing. He puts the bowl down, washes his hands and rises from his seat to look for them.

Outside his tent, there is a woman, riding up on a royal horse.

6 Traditional compressed rice cakes commonly served with peanut-sauce dishes or sweets.

Long Zahir recognises her instantly. She is the messenger-woman from Istana Meranti. She has come to deliver a message, from Long Jaafar, the King, and does not stay long to watch Kitang read it aloud from the paper scroll.

Long Zahir guesses the main contents of the letter – Si Larut has not yet returned to the palace, and the king is gravely anxious about it.

Kitang passes the scroll to Long Zahir. He gives Long Zahir a rare, gainful smile, which readily fades as his gaze flits down to the scroll. The *jawi*[7] words glitter under the moonlight. From afar, it looks like tiny earthworms squirming in ruler-straight rows.

"He wants us to find Si Larut in just … two more days?" The penmanship sends red-hot anger which engulfs his cheeks, making the veins in his neck pulse stronger. He reads the other parts of the text aloud. "It is predicted a flash flood will hit the palace if Si Larut is dead …"

* * *

Not far from the tent, Rembulan is pouring water over Senduduk's body.

Senduduk, under the moonlight, stands as a silent sentinel watching the men. She stretches out her trunk as if she wants to catch the full moon.

"*Lot*!" utters Rembulan curtly. It means "lower your head". Senduduk blinks for a few seconds before brandishing her ivory tusks downwards.

"Have you eaten?" Long Zahir's voice resonates like he is speaking into a hollow bamboo. Rembulan nods briefly.

"Sorry, *Tuan*. I've failed you. I've brought a curse upon the palace because of not taking good care of Si Larut."

7 A writing system used for writing the Malay language and several other languages of Southeast Asia based on the Arabic script.

"It's just a threat from the palace. I don't believe in such superstition. The only minister in the palace that I trust is Kitang. That's why I brought him here to guide us to find Si Larut."

"*Tuan*, the king is not happy about this. I've failed this time. If we can't locate Si Larut in two days' time, I'll be punished." Rembulan's gut feels like it is tightened by thorny vines. He has heard all the stories, of how slaves are severely punished for being incompetent or disobedient.

> **Three so-called debt-slaves – a boy and three girls, all under twenty years of age, had escaped from the house and custody of the Sultan, and run away … The boy was taken into a field and kris-ed.**
>
> **– Sir Frank Athelstane Swettenham**, *The Real Malay*

"No, I won't allow it. I'm to be blamed as well. I rode Si Larut that evening without my father's consent. It's my fault, too, that I didn't put on the *singkla*[8] properly. I've promised him to bring Si Larut back. And, we'll bring him back."

"*Terum puan*!" Rembulan orders Senduduk curtly. She trumpets briefly, bends her front knees to touch the sandy ground, then gravitates her body downwards skilfully behind them. Upon sensing the warmth of her leathery skin, Long Zahir and Rembulan recline their backs against her.

> **Malay elephant-drivers, in directing their beasts, use a kind of elephant language, which comes from Siam, and seems to be understood by the animals.**
>
> **– Sir Frank Athelstane Swettenham**, *The Real Malay*

Senduduk lives up to her name. She roars like an untamed lion, sending waves of tremors throughout the Malay Peninsula.

8 A piece of equipment to shackle an elephant.

Senduduk is a reincarnation of ancient animal spirits. Not even a wall of men and horses can stop her if she is to run amok. Only men of royal blood could rein a beast like that. Si Larut is her son, one of Long Jaafar's princely possessions. Si Larut is often displayed at royal weddings, coronations and opening ceremonies of local mining sites.

"In time, the wild elephants will see through our strategy. They'll attack us again, if we let them," Rembulan says soberly.

Words of caution fail to dampen Long Zahir's heavily-spirited mind and body.

"Sip the nipa sugar juice and enjoy the night. You worry too much." Long Zahir then rests his head on Rembulan's lap. He closes his eyes slowly, secretly enjoying the warmth.

"*Tuan*, you must rest in your tent," Rembulan spreads open a sarong and covers Long Zahir's bare chest. Red lines criss-cross over his sternum. A bruised patch marks his lower right chest, possibly hiding a cracked rib.

"It's hot in there. Besides, I can take care of Senduduk and the other elephants. Kitang is inspecting the bamboo grove with the men. We'll take turns to guard the elephants tonight." Long Zahir clasps Rembulan's right hand and lays it firmly on his chest.

Like Long Zahir, Senduduk closes her eyes too, possibly learning to fly in her dream. Rembulan then peers into the distance. Men are still toiling to make camp while some struggle to pound the pungent *ketub-ketub* roots into a mushy pulp, before feeding it to the elephants as a nutritional supplement.

> **We take a considerable quantity of the roots of *ketub-ketub* and *panggil-panggil* and pound them into pulp, and give them to the elephant in his food for three consecutive mornings or evenings. This is certain to make the elephant courageous.**

– **W George Maxwell**, *Mantra Gajah*

Cicadas screech in nearby bushes. Frogs in singsong vocals beg for a downpour. Rembulan turns his head to face Mount Korbu, which is cloaked in a greenish and purplish haze.

Rembulan admires Long Zahir's determination to learn the art of elephant language from him and Kitang. Only a week with the elephants and he can order them around effortlessly. Commanding elephants is a tedious task. The commands are mere short phrases in Siamese. The commands will be ignored by the elephants if the learner is not patient enough to synchronise eye contact, voice tone and body language while talking with them.

Long Zahir has fallen asleep on Rembulan's lap. His face is calm despite the stinging blisters all over his body. Even a prince is not immune to insect bites.

* * *

"Shh! He's there! He's alone." Kitang signals the men behind him.

As expected, Si Larut towers over the bushes in the marshy compound, still with his soiled *songket*[9] caparison. He lifts his trunk several times mid-air, as if worshipping the morning sun.

Long Zahir keeps his back straight, hands folded and eagle eyes looking forward. Rembulan struggles to do the same. He envies his master's ease in upholding that relentlessly firm strength.

"Listen, let's end this. We'll settle this once and for all today. We'll bring Si Larut back before those wild elephants return!" Long Zahir sharpens his gaze.

Kitang enchants a Siamese war cry. His voice booms, even with no intent to shout: "O, the Mandate of Heaven, give me strength

9 A fabric that belongs to the brocade family of textiles of the Malay world. It is handwoven in silk or cotton, and intricately patterned with gold or silver threads.

and wisdom to command the elephants. My body is the vessel for your divinity."

Long Zahir's smile is bowstring-tight and mirthless. His eyes light up with exhilaration on unsheathing his kris.[10] "Our five-day expedition will end today. There'll be no bloodshed anymore."

"Bring out only the female elephants. Rembulan, prepare the rattan nooses!" Kitang outlines his plan while eyeing Si Larut walk towards a small river.

Along the river bank, Si Larut is induced to join the society of the three female elephants which are let loose on purpose. He moves forward, sprinkling water on each one of them. Together, they feed on the sprouting sugar canes nearby. Not far from them, on the ground, in some convenient place between two trees, rattan nooses with ordinary running knots lay quietly on the ground.

"*Dee dee! Dee dee! Dee dee!*" A group of men calls out the command words a good stone's throw away from the elephants. All three female elephants respond immediately to the command. It means "come here now". They abandon the place and start climbing up the river bank. As predicted, Si Larut follows them from behind. Seizing this good sign, the men form a barricade around them, forcing them towards the site of the nooses.

Urged by the tense environment, Si Larut plants his foot unknowingly into a noose. Rembulan and the men pull the knot and he is caught immediately. He trumpets short regretful screeches and advances a few sluggish steps forward, attempting to free himself. The end of the line fastened to the noose is attached to a heavy mass of leafy branches and acts as a drag to slow his movement. Fatigue soon makes him move slower. His mother, Senduduk, and another female elephant sandwich him on both sides. Kitang then binds all three of them into a set.

10 An Indonesian asymmetrical dagger.

An elephant, whether caught with a herd or a noose, is kept tied up until it has been thoroughly subdued and quiet, and will submit to being washed and handled.

– W George Maxwell, *Mantra Gajah.*

* * *

"*Ayahanda,*[11] please forgive Rembulan. I need him. He has been working for me for two years. His loyalty is not to be questioned. He's a good *gambala*[12] and has taught me many elephant words. My training with the elephants has not yet been completed," pleads Long Zahir. He has been sitting on the cushioned altar for almost an hour. Rembulan kneels behind him, on the bare floor, shirtless, with his wrists shackled behind his neck. "*Ayahanda,* he has helped us to track Si Larut, too."

Long Jaafar, despite having Si Larut returned safely, is still keen to punish Rembulan for his recklessness.

And somehow, as his heart wrenches, Rembulan feels that Long Zahir is genuine in his plea. He hangs his head low.

"*Ampun Tuanku,*"[13] Kitang saunters into the chamber with a pair of royal guards.

"Yes, Kitang. What good prophecies have come across your mind today? I'm still thinking about the best punishment to give this Siamese slave of mine." Long Jaafar turns his face towards Kitang.

"*Ampun Tuanku.* The washers found this black sand from Si Larut's breast collar. I think this is what the Siamese call *timah.*" Kitang opens up a piece of folded cloth, revealing black grains of sand.

"Is that true?" Long Jaafar hurries down excitedly from his

11 A poetic term for father or a senior male relative in Malay.

12 A herdsman in Malay.

13 Literally means "begging your indulgence", in an archaic form of the Malay language, from a subject addressing the sultan (royal ruler) of a Malay state.

throne and palpates the grainy-textured sand. Elated, he then sniffs at the mixture repetitively, almost blackening the tip of his nose.

"Oh! Oh! My *Anakanda*[14] Zahir," Long Jaafar turns around quickly.

"Yes, *Ayahanda*?"

"Unshackle that slave. You can keep him forever. I've granted him my pardon on one condition."

"Tell me the condition, *Ayahanda*."

"Bring him with you to find the source of this special mud. This is *biji timah*.[15] It's very precious. It must be from the swampy area where you found Si Larut. I'll send men to guard you from the wild elephants. Talk to Si Larut in whatever language you want, and make sure he shows us the right place."

It is on record that, by 1844, tin was exported to Penang from Larut.

– **Khoo Kay Kim**, *Taiping (Larut): The Early History of a Mining Settlement*

Author's Note

Many months ago, I came across a posting on Twitter discussing the art of talking to elephants by Malay herdsmen in Perak, a state in Malaysia. I was instantly captivated by such a tradition which is obviously no longer a practice nowadays.

I did some research on the issue and found out that the claim was not fictitious at all. Several English authors, such as Sir Frank Athelstane Swettenham and particularly W George Maxwell, a former British colonial administrator of British Malaya, have written extensively on this matter.

14 A poetic term for son or younger male/female relative in Malay.
15 Tin in Malay.

Impressed by the uniqueness of this practice, I decided to write short stories or essays as a way to preserve this long-lost heritage. Hopefully, through works of fiction, I can highlight the beauty of such an art and integrate some elements of this early 19th century practice into Malay society.

While planning for my story, I realised that writing about a group of men talking to elephants is not easy. I needed a strong story arc, which I found when I read about the real case of a missing elephant from a journal article on the early history of the mining settlement in Perak. I used this incident as the foundation for the plot of my story. The story is set in early 19th century Perak in British Malaya, where the tin ore trade began to flourish.

In my story, the characters give a specialised set of commands to instruct the elephants to do a specific task, as described by W George Maxwell in his book *Mantra Gajah*. This usage of the command phrases makes the story extremely realistic and unique. Other minor issues that I have woven into the story relate to human-animal relationship, slavery, animal hunting and abuse and the exploitation of natural resources.

Excerpts from books and a journal are integrated into the story. This creative technique is deployed in order to give further background information on a particular scene or event.

Lotus Flower

Alice Bianchi-Clark

Buddhism is prevalent in Thailand and most temples are Buddhist. The Buddhists believe that when Buddha took his first steps into the mortal world, lotus blooms blossomed under his bare feet. That's why whether he is reclining, standing or sitting, Buddha is always portrayed on a lotus flower.

The lotus is a symbol of purity because it emerges from the mud to rise in the water. It is a sacred flower. Its pink-tinted white and short-lived blooms are scented. Its seed pods are sculptural. Its large, velvety, umbrella-like leaves are waterproof. In Thailand, the dead are honoured with incense sticks and lotus flowers. Monks wear saffron-coloured robes and often chant in temples. All footwear must be removed before entering temple precincts. White silk is widely worn for funerals. Tuk-tuks are motorised versions of rickshaws with open seating for passengers. Tuk-tuk rides in Bangkok are no longer as prevalent as they used to be.

Most children grow up with a few books, some with a few shelves; she grew up in a library.

Her destiny seemed sealed when she was brought back from the hospital, wailing. The fated placement of her Moses basket was, in all honesty, an afterthought. She had popped out a full four weeks early and in the tearful confusion that ensued, Father tucked the Moses basket under hovering shelves, until arrangements could be made to dispel the disquiet that had followed her stormy arrival.

Father's sister, Aunt Laetitia, flew into Bangkok with hairpins dangling from her golden hair and in quintessential British style, hired a nanny, whose exemplary qualifications would have made Mary Poppins sniff with approval. Aunt Laetitia had an English country manor to manage back in Herefordshire, including two whippets and a husband, so she could not extend her stay indefinitely. Her maternal grandparents, *Khun Tah*[1] and *Khun Yai,*[2] moved in instead, with *Mae-baan,*[3] their trusted helper. They called Father *Khun Por,*[4] and the baby Ubon. The British nanny soon vanished, possibly on a gust of westerly wind, and Mother's plans for the nursery were abandoned.

Yet, even as a baby, Ubon knew better than to fuss. She soon outgrew the basket, which was replaced by a cot. Eventually, her cot was replaced by a small bed. In turn, that too was replaced by a lime green armchair, which stretched into a single bed at night and curled back into a cocoon during the daytime – *rather like a caterpillar*, Ubon thought.

The hazardous shelves overhead, on the contrary, became permanent fixtures, in spite of *Khun Tah*, *Khun Yai* and *Mae-baan's* protests. More were added above and all around, until all the walls were wallpapered with the jumbled, variegated spines of the books Father collected. Wherever she looked, there were shelves piled alongside and upon one another – *like the layers of a humongous sponge cake*, Ubon thought.

As soon as she was old enough to read, Ubon started devouring the stories that made up her room, spine by spine, illustration by illustration. Barefoot, legs kicking in the air, she would lay on her belly for hours on the faded, peacock green rug with patterns fanning out like many tails. The characters in her books were the siblings she'd never had, the pets she'd never befriended – their adventures wilder than any in her imagination.

The tall window in her library was the most welcome fixture, because from where she liked to stand on tiptoe, on a pile of books,

---

1 "Khun" is a respectful Thai term for addressing family members, while "Tah" is the Thai word for maternal grandfather.

2 "Yai" is the Thai word for maternal grandmother.

3 "Mae" is the Thai word for mother. "Baan" is the Thai word for house. "Mae-baan" is Thai for a live-in helper.

4 "Por" is the Thai word for father.

it seemed to frame the city's snaking river and skyscrapers, vying vertiginously – *stepping stones to the clouds*, Ubon thought.

"Cordelia?"

A dainty beaded slipper peeped in between the terracotta pots and disappeared. Only her aunt called her by her first name, her British name. Ubon looked up, but sitting where she was, behind the rickety table, she went unnoticed.

Father's bare, gentle feet padded onto the stone slabs. He was absent-minded, except when he was tending his prized lotuses, which flowered in water-filled pots around the perimeter of their balcony. As accustomed as she was to his silence, Ubon enjoyed the proximity to Father and often sat among the lotuses, spying on him – *playing peek-a-boo*, Ubon thought.

She dipped her fingers in the murky water, tempting the guppy fish to nibble at her fingertips. She was envious of the hours Father liked to spend undisturbed, weeding and humming. It seemed so unfair, given the lotuses thrived regardless of his attention.

"Oh, there you are," Aunt Laetitia said, laying down her tray. She stooped over a lotus flower, held it to her nose and sniffed. Ubon crinkled hers; the heady scent of lotus flowers was an unwelcome reminder of Mother's absence.

Ubon much preferred the unscented lotus seed pods. There was something so architectural about them, where their seeds became gateways to multiple possibilities.

Aunt Laetitia busied herself with setting out the delicate cups and delectable treats. She invited Father to sit at the table.

Father's blonde hair was greying, his cheeks were gaunt, and his mouth set into a perennial, stiff line, which he rubbed with his forefinger. He looked at the white blooms as if enchanted by a nostalgic memory.

"I'm enamoured with all my gardens, Gerald," said Aunt Laetitia, "but I must say your balcony is utterly charming. There's something so healing about these lotus flowers. I understand why she loved them so."

Ubon longed to hear stories about her mother. She yearned to find out who she was. *Khun Tah* and *Khun Yai* were not storytellers, and Father was, well, Father.

His blue eyes were transfixed on a proud stalk with its protective, velvety, umbrella-like leaves – *so like Father*, Ubon thought.

"She would be so proud of you, Gerald."

Father stiffened.

"How I wish I could persuade both of you to come to England, but she is the reason you are still here after all these years. Gerald?"

A swallow flew past, tracing figures of eight above Ubon's head. Even Ubon knew Bangkok was Mother's hometown.

* * *

Most children look forward to their birthdays but not Ubon. Every year, she wished she could curl asleep and wake up a day later so as to skip it altogether. She detested the rituals they honoured that day, the cumbersome, sticky white silks they wore to the temple and the jolting, hair-tangling tuk-tuk ride. She loathed how the monks' incessant chanting buzzed in her ears, the dusty stone slabs blackened the soles of her bare feet, the smoky incense blurred her eyes, and the heady smell of the lotus flowers, which they invariably brought as offerings, triggered a choking sensation.

"*Khun Mae*'s favourite," *Khun Yai* said, referring to Mother. "When Buddha took his first steps into the mortal world, lotus blooms blossomed under his bare feet."

Ubon knew how sacred lotuses were in Thailand, and how they grew abundant in and out of temples and among Buddhist statuary. Still, hot tears streamed down her cheeks. Mother's spirit was omnipresent and suffocating. Ubon wanted to tear away from it but, wherever she darted and leapt, she missed, as if she were trying to catch onto her own shadow.

Khun Yai perched next to her on the steps of the temple, as if she thought herself a bird, rather than an over-adorned elephant. Her gold bangles chimed.

"That's why whether he is reclining, standing or sitting, Buddha is always portrayed on a lotus," she said, offering Ubon a tissue.

Khun Tah and *Khun Yai* were as constant in their love as they were content. They never expressed their sadness or anger. Nothing seemed to upset them, whereas everything upsets Ubon. If she hadn't been born, Mother might still be alive and Father would not look so displaced or forlorn.

Khun Yai smiled, like one of the Buddha statues she venerated, and repeated, "*Mai bpen rai*."[5] It was her favourite expression: she used it for everything, for cuts and grazes, spilt coconut milk and on Ubon's birthdays.

Only Aunt Laetitia seemed determined not to let Mother's death mar Ubon's special day. She would bake her a strawberry cream cake, play "Happy Birthday" on the piano and bring lots of ribbon-wrapped presents filled with frilly taffeta dresses and impractical satin shoes wrapped in scented tissue paper.

"Remember you're half-British, Cordelia," she'd say with pride, as if the British half were the better half – even Ubon knew that couldn't be so.

* * *

Father kept to himself. *Khun Tah* and *Khun Yai* never questioned how they all lived together but apart. When he was not lavishing his attention on his blooms, Father was happiest when absorbed in a storybook or when the doorbell rang with a delivery of books in a brown cardboard box. The living room was soon filled with

5 A Thai expression used to denote that things are as they are and making one's peace with the situation is the best way to move forward.

shelves. Ubon didn't mind; the books brought colour to the walls and the windows provided the changeable artwork – subject to weather patterns and the occasional flight of birds.

Ubon loved how Father often read to her after work and way past her bedtime. He had an expressive voice and best impersonated feverish dragons, cantankerous ogres and formidable stepmothers. Ubon relished the way his voice faltered when he was moved, how his eyes popped, goldfish style, to underline innocent astonishment and how he waved his arm with a graceful flourish or tapped his fingers whenever the pace of a story quickened. She loved how he called her "bonbon" and ruffled her hair and stroked it, in a way that was not allowed in Thai culture. Ubon's only experience of love, joy and grief was through stories, for it was through stories that Father best expressed his love.

"What does Cordelia do in that library all day?" asked Aunt Laetitia. "The girl needs an education, Gerald." She wrung her hands and the gems on her fingers caught the light and sparkled.

Even Ubon knew what Aunt Laetitia meant by an education. Although she was older than her father, Aunt Laetitia was still surprisingly glamorous and svelte, and when she waltzed into their cosy apartment trailing her expensive, inebriating scent of damask rose behind her. Her coquettish chatter filled the air so that Ubon couldn't hear herself think. In Aunt Laetitia's mind, of course, the only worthy education was in the art of womanhood. She had either buried or divorced three husbands, and was determined to swindle a fourth out of his fortune before it could fast diminish.

"The girl has all the education she needs, Letty," said Father, brandishing his penknife to prise open yet another musty cardboard box – which in Ubon's imagination, became an oversized seashell in which to hide.

"She's even taught herself how to read. Haven't you, bonbon?" he said with a wink. Ubon noticed how his thin chest seemed to puff out a little. Father so relished an opportunity to banter with and wind up his sister that one corner of his mouth curled upwards. Ubon knew he secretly loved the way Aunt Laetitia fussed about him because so did she.

"Cordelia would be quite fetching – if only you'd let me have my way with her," Aunt Laetitia said with a petulant pout. "With those dark, wide, doe-shaped eyes, her silky, long black hair, Busaba's radiant skin …"

Aunt Laetitia's voice faltered and Ubon noticed how her father winced at the mention of Mother as if the memory haunted him still. She pictured her mother's sepia photograph with the gold headdress and contrived upturned hands of the traditional Thai dancer she'd been.

Aunt Laetitia sighed with exasperation. Her pearl drop earrings quivered. Her skirt rustled. Her fan flapped. "Oh, Cordelia, what do you have to say about all this?" she said, with a despairing gesture at the infinite shelves of books.

Ubon knew better than to reply. She ran off to find *Khun Yai* but could not locate her, and settled for the next best thing by crawling under Father's emptied cardboard box.

"I've booked the Mandarin Oriental for a spot of afternoon tea. You have to see the dress I picked up for her in Paris, Gerald," Aunt Laetitia simpered. "It's divine."

Ubon held her breath under the cardboard box and listened. She didn't want to wear another dress with ribbons that got caught everywhere and an itchy tulle underskirt; or have her hair yanked into plaits and her scalp prodded with pins, not even for her beloved and only aunt.

"Oh Gerald, let us sit on your darling balcony until she reappears," she said, as if only the blooms could assuage her distress.

Father chuckled. "She's not a doll. She's a reader," he said with pride.

Those kind, promising words filled Ubon's soul like warm air fills the silk canopy of a hot-air balloon. No wonder she read so voraciously after that. When he found her immersed in a book, Father would tiptoe around her. Ubon sensed that he looked at her differently too, the way he admired his lotus buds before they bloomed.

* * *

"Cordelia Ubon Chatsworth?" repeated the headmaster, when Cordelia was first introduced to him. For it was during one of Aunt Laetitia's whirlwind visits that the question of her schooling was settled. "Cordelia, what an unusual name."

"'*Cor*' is Latin for courage ..." said Aunt Laetitia, gushing.

"Heart," corrected Ubon under her breath.

"From 'A Midsummer Night's Dream'," said Aunt Laetitia.

"'King Lear', actually," murmured Ubon.

Aunt Laetitia frowned. She added, with an emphatic flourish of her fan, "My brother is devoted to Shakespeare ..."

"Aren't we all?" said the headmaster, with a nod of approval.

Why do adults so spurn correction? They certainly relish correcting us children, Ubon thought.

"I'm Baroness Willoughby, Cordelia's aunt," she said, offering her hand limply, as if she were used to having it kissed rather than shaken. "Cordelia, darling," she added, tilting her head.

As if on cue, Ubon extracted her book from her satchel. She was grateful for any excuse to read about Mr Darcy. She suspected Miss Bennet had been mistaken about him.

"It's about Cordelia's admission. Currently, Cordelia attends a darling little local school, but I'm persuaded she would thrive with more structure. My brother is so consumed with his work, he's researching his next biography, and well, I thought I'd make myself useful. I fear when it comes to choosing a suitable school in the tropics, one able to match the academic rigours required of an Eng …" she hesitated, "an enviable institution," – although Ubon was certain she'd meant to say "English" – "… a woman's touch is required. You do understand, don't you?"

Ubon had learnt to read between the lines, for not much was ever said at home, but she wondered how well the headmaster could do so. She loved the school *Khun Yai* had chosen.

However, she was grateful when Father refused to send her to a boarding school in England, and instead settled for a British colonial education, as Aunt Laetitia put it.

* * *

"She's uninterested in her peers. Most lunchtimes, she'll be hiding under some table. We cannot seem to get her nose out of a book." Ubon overheard her teacher say at one parent-teacher evening. "Do you understand, Mr Chatsworth?"

There was a pause. Ubon felt her cheeks blush. Through the glass partition, Ubon felt the teacher's stare and was careful not to draw attention to herself by looking over the rim of her book. Elephantine *Khun Yai* sat resting with her eyes closed. "*Mai bpen rai*," she whispered, as if she knew.

"Mr Chatsworth, I urge you to take your daughter's education seriously."

There was another pause. Ubon huddled closer to *Khun Yai*; her warm body was so comforting. She tried to concentrate on her book – if only Jo March could find it in her heart to accept Laurie.

"Surely, the struggle with children nowadays is how to dissuade them from technological distractions. You claim you cannot get my daughter's nose out of a book. I'm not sure if *you* understand." Father spoke in a soft, courteous voice, but even Ubon could sense his exasperation.

"Mr Chatsworth ..."

"Have you considered the benefits of entrusting her with some good old-fashioned social responsibility?"

"There are friendship captains, environmentalists, class and year representatives ..."

"How about the school library?" Father said.

* * *

That was how Ubon slid into her first job, unpaid, but a job nevertheless. She fitted in effortlessly. She loved the musty smell of it, the quietness, the orderliness, the rustling of turned pages and the books arranged in alphabetical order and by subject, just like her own.

The librarian, Mrs Wordsworth, petted Ubon as if she knew how hard kindred spirits were to come by. She would peer at her over the top rim of her bifocals, unaware of the way she nodded approvingly, whenever Ubon aligned the spines along the shelf just so or taped up the torn pages of books – l*ike a loving vet administering bandages*, Ubon thought.

By now, Ubon wore thick, round glasses – glasses too heavy for a girl her age – and she enjoyed peering in and out of them as if through a looking glass. She loved the fact that Mrs Wordsworth understood, instinctively, that her shyness originated not from any anxiety, narcissism or self-absorption, but from her difficulty in reading people. The characters in her books made infinitely more sense to her because on paper, she could read their thoughts, and empathise with their feelings and motivations; their adventures were hers to appropriate as her own, if only she was willing to read on.

"I sometimes wonder about you," said Mrs Wordsworth.

Ubon knew what Mrs Wordsworth meant by that remark. If Ubon had been a character in one of her books, Ubon would have been described as laconic. It's not that she didn't have anything to say, rather, she was careful with her choice of words and used them sparingly.

"You do love to read, don't you?" asked Mrs Wordsworth, peering at her.

Ubon nodded. She was grateful that Mrs Wordsworth only ever asked rhetorical questions; she talked to her as if she were a pet.

"Artists use lines, shapes and colour to view the world," said Mrs Wordsworth, "but words can be so empowering, can't they?"

"And heartless," Ubon murmured.

Mrs Wordsworth sat down on a stool and laid her knobbly hand on Ubon's shoulder, as if to encourage her to elaborate.

"Words hurled in anger wound, undermine and negate the feelings of others but," Ubon hesitated, "thoughtless words are most cruel."

Mrs Wordsworth leaned towards Ubon. Reverently, she steepled her fingers and pursed her lips as if to savour Ubon's words.

"Reading is so healing. It cultivates compassion."

There was a sparkle in Mrs Wordsworth's eyes; it betrayed how much she revelled in the guileless geniality of Ubon's insight. She waited as if to ensure there was nothing more forthcoming.

"You must find reading most therapeutic, dear child," said Mrs Wordsworth.

* * *

Aunt Laetitia, on the other hand, lamented over this. "All Cordelia does is read," she whined.

It's the only way I know how to make sense of the world, Ubon wished to say.

Father didn't take his eyes off his book but still managed to imbue his words with, if not genuine surprise, then surely the pretence of it. "She does like to read, doesn't she?"

"Oh, Gerald, look at her! She's so frightened of life. What will Cordelia do at university?"

Ubon dreaded leaving Thailand; it was all she knew. Yet, she was curious about England.

"I firmly suspect that she'll ..." a half grin appeared on Father's face, "... keep reading. I understand that's what's expected of literature graduates."

"Oh Gerald, be serious."

"Have you read any of the books she's read?"

Aunt Laetitia flapped her opulent sleeves.

"I take that as a no," Father said, arching his eyebrows.

Ubon held her breath. She had loved reading her father's books. She imagined he'd left a fragment of himself in each one and had trusted her to gather up the pieces.

Father winked at the door approvingly, as if he had expected Ubon to be spying them through the keyhole all along. "If the books we read make us who we are, she has all the prerequisites to be sensational."

"Oh, Gerald," Aunt Laetitia whimpered.

"Children don't need our worries, Letty. They need us to believe in them," said Father, closing his book emphatically and resting it on the coffee table.

"Is that all?"

"Absolutely. Her life will be full of joy, Letty."

"How can you be so sure?"

He cleared his throat then, as if to help him enunciate his words and project them far and wide, so that they might be heard from the other side of the door. "She knows the truth."

"What truth, Gerald?"

Bangles jingled. Ubon turned to see *Khun Yai* nod before lolloping away. If she had noticed Ubon eavesdropping, she pretended not to.

"Read for joy – no other reason is as compelling," Father said.

"And what truth is that?"

He grinned. "Mine."

Indeed, Ubon was compelled to read: she read for herself, to make sense of who she was, to find her place in the world. She craved love and connection. She longed to feel at one with humanity.

"She certainly doesn't need fixing, Letty."

No, Ubon thought. If *Khun Tah* or *Khun Yai* had been anxious about Ubon's future, they never let it on. Unlike Aunt Laetitia, who couldn't help conniving and strategising, they trusted in the healing power of love. Now Ubon felt the full force of Father's love too – pure and unconditional. It gave her strength, it buoyed her. There was a knot in her throat. *Am I enough as I am?*

"Marriage may fix your problems, not Ubon's. She longs for romance ..."

Aunt Laetitia had just remarried – her fifth marriage – and had yet to comprehend why this marriage, which had done wonders for her finances, had been unable to quench her need for love.

She snorted. "I was always misguided about marriage. I was just frightened of feeling lonely."

"You have us, don't you?" Father rested a hand on hers.

Aunt Laetitia's blue, bewildered eyes were teary. "Oh!" She sniffed.

You do, thought Ubon.

"You, on the other hand, suited marriage, like in one of your storybooks. I know you don't like to talk about it, Gerald, but it was an accident ..."

"I should have insisted on a hospital delivery in London."

"You respected her wishes. Busaba never wanted to leave Thailand. She honoured family and tradition."

"It was my fault ..."

"No, Gerald. She developed eclampsia. Even with the best

doctors, she might have passed away. Busaba wanted to give birth here. This is her home. That's why you raised Cordelia here. Every day you stay, you honour Busaba."

Ubon knew now why she couldn't leave Thailand. She hadn't come to terms with the rippling effects of Mother's absence.

"That child needs you to talk about her mother," Aunt Laetitia said. "Don't you see her mother is the key to understanding who she is?"

Ubon gulped. *Mother was the missing fragment.*

"Cordelia blames her birth for her mother's death and your unhappiness, Gerald."

Once voiced, Ubon's secret no longer felt shameful. She held it in the palm of her hand and felt the smarting pain burn with renewed intensity. Although the anguish didn't ebb away, it became bearable and meaningful – her anguish, a measure of her love's endurance.

Father reached out for his sister as if there was a knot in his throat, too. "Oh, Letty!"

Ubon felt at one with Father's deep-seated pain, tugging at the silk canopy of her half-filled hot-air balloon, like a wicker basket struggling to take flight.

Aunt Laetitia took Father's hand and kissed it. "The only thing I blame you for is losing hope after she passed away."

"But I didn't. I find hope here in my books ... in my flowers."

Hot tears streamed down Ubon's cheeks; if only Father had found hope in her.

"What about Cordelia? Don't you see? Reading is a way to you. All you ever cared about were books and flowers. She wants to read so that she can connect with you and your anguish, and understand her own." Her forehead was corrugated with the kind of deep creases she had spent years plumping up with costly anti-wrinkle potions, but Ubon loved her best then. For once, she was not fretting. Love was everywhere, binding them together like a girdle.

"She is my …" Father's voice faltered. His eyes had that intense look he reserved for his treasured lotus buds. "… Come, Letty. There's something I want to show you."

"What is it?"

Ubon read Father' lips. He mouthed her name.

"I beg your pardon?"

"Lotus is a symbol of purity because it emerges from the mud to rise in the water. That's why Busaba called her daughter Ubon, lotus flower."

Ubon turned her back to the door and slid down against it. She looked up to the ceiling and closed her eyes. Her mother's presence glowed; it warmed her. She listened. *Khun Yai*'s words lullabied her on, "*Mai bpen rai, mai bpen rai, mai bpen rai* …" *Things are as they are*, she thought.

She heard Father's footsteps withdrawing. She imagined Father stepping onto their balcony, among the delicate, tall lotus buds yearning and stretching instinctively towards the sunlight.

Author's Note

I believe that writing should be honest and true, no matter how close to the heart. For it is through vulnerability that humans best connect.

I've always fantasised writing about a character who grew up in a library. I also grew up in a library, although I never called it that – it was my bedroom. My family lived in a small apartment in central Rome. When I was born, the library was turned into my bedroom, with floor to ceiling bookshelves. Bookshelves hovered above my bed and were also tucked away under my window just like in Ubon's room. I wondered what a child, who calls her bedroom a library, might grow up to be.

Mrs Wordsworth is modelled on the inspirational librarian I worked with at Trinity Hall in Cambridge. I have fond memories of sharing tea and shortbread with her overlooking the River Cam while discussing literature. I sometimes wonder how my life would be if I had studied English literature at university instead of law. For this reason, Ubon's father embraces Ubon's interest in literature. He also firmly believes that there is no other reason for reading other than for the sheer joy of it.

In terms of technique, I aim for sensory descriptions. I start with what I see and then add sounds, smells, sometimes taste and touch. I prefer strong verbs. I use plenty of adjectives but use adverbs sparingly. For example, with Aunt Laetitia, who is well groomed, fashionable and forever fretting, I describe her through her dress and accessories. She is a whirlwind and moves like one: she waltzes in, her fan flaps, her skirt rustles, her pearl drop earrings quiver, the gems on her fingers sparkle as they catch the light, her scent is inebriating.

Khun Yai instead represents calm serenity. Her love is constant. Her description is pared down and brings to mind pachyderms. The sound associated with her is the chiming of a bangle because it has a reverberating resonance rather than a dissonant clanking sound.

I like to weave layers into my writing to give it more depth, for example, in a dialogue scene I first write out all the words the characters will say, then I go back and add actions. Each time I go back, I add something different: body language, visceral reactions, thoughts and descriptions.

Picking out the Stones

Heidi Emily Eusebio-Abad

Filipinos are known for having closely-knit families. It is not unusual for grown-up children to continue living with their parents, even if the children have gotten married and are already raising their own families. In fact, the parents, now grandparents, may even end up being taken care of by the younger generation. Aside from this expansion of the nuclear family, it is not surprising to extend the household to the unmarried aunts or uncles of the clan. Mutual beneficial relations are formed when the senior members help with babysitting the young, or when the young and able provide caregiving for the invalid elders of the family. In the process, a single household with enough room to spare in their property may even build additional rooms or living quarters for the extended members of the family.

This multi-generational set-up also helps in preserving some of the cultural practices and beliefs of Filipinos. *Mano po* is a polite and respectful greeting to elders which is accompanied by the taking of their hand and touching it to one's forehead, at the same time bowing for an easier reach. Even the simplest family habits may be passed on to the next generation by mere exposure to the routines of the elders.

The best part of a multi-generational household is when stories of each generation's life experiences are shared among family members. Stories about wartime survival, school pranks, birthday celebrations, family outings and even memories of loved ones long gone, help to strengthen the bonds of family love.

"She's picking out the stones again, as usual," my younger brother, Jun-jun, snickers as he peeks through the screened window of Tiya Tinay's[1] kitchen.

"Get out of there before she sees you!" I hiss.

1 "Tiya" means aunt in Tagalog; a variation of the term "Tita".

Jun-jun crouches and sneaks through the *sampaguita*[2] bushes planted along the back wall of Auntie's house.

"Yup! She's at it again at exactly 9am without fail." My brother giggles as he skips his way back to our house in the family compound.

Our compound is made up of three different households, each with its own modest bungalow surrounded by a great many old trees and a common front yard that gets littered with dried leaves every time the wind blows.

The house closest to the driveway leading to the front gate of the compound belongs to *Tatay*'s[3] younger sister, Tita Neneng[4] and her husband. I have six first cousins – all boys – stirring up a mess in that house. Theirs is a noisy household with the stereo blasting out the latest hip-hop tunes downloaded by the three older teens, doors opening and slamming shut, and, of course, the squealing voices of the three younger kids still in the primary grades. It's a happy kind of riot, which is why my pubescent brother likes hanging out there.

My family occupies what we call the middle house. It's not really in the middle of the compound. In fact, the house hugs the west wall of the compound where most of the trees are planted. We get very little sunlight because of the tall wall and the trees. I like it, though. The noise of the front house is buffered. I prefer quiet. Jun-jun calls it my "emo self". Sometimes, he teases me by saying that I'd probably end up like our grumpy, old-maid-of-an-auntie who lives in the house at the back.

Tiya Tinay is *Tatay*'s eldest sister. She prefers the title *Tiya* to *Tita*, which she considers too pretentious as it is used more by socialites. She used to live with us in our house but when my younger brother was born, she insisted on converting the old

2 A scented tropical flower, a species of jasmine, native to Asia and the national flower of the Philippines.

3 Father in Tagalog.

4 "Tita" means aunt in Tagalog; also a respectful term for addressing older women.

bodega[5] at the back into a small house for her. It was a suitable reuse of storage space for old things or old people.

* * *

"He's cute now," she said, "because he's a newborn. Wait a few weeks. Wait a couple more years. He'll turn into a noisy, naughty boy with endless energy. See those boys of Neneng. *Haaay*! What that will do to my nerves, my high blood pressure!"

That said, *Tatay* and a carpenter who used to work on our house converted the old *bodega* into a cozy cottage for Tiya Tinay.

"Nice house," *Tatay* exclaimed when they were done. Tiya Tinay only raised an eyebrow, shrugged and proceeded to carry her packed luggage into the newly-refurbished *bodega* house, as we secretly called it.

"This will do," was all she said as her way of thanking my father.

Some months after Tiya Tinay moved out of our house, it turned out she was right. My cute little brother morphed into a cute little prankster with endless energy. Sometimes, when he got too hyperactive for me to handle and constantly invaded my private space, I wished *I* was the occupant of the *bodega* house.

* * *

I've just had my moving-up ceremony in school, from junior high to senior high school. This is the summer for me to enjoy the beach with friends. Or maybe the summer to attend the young writers' workshop in Baguio.[6] Or maybe just go "malling" by myself and hang out in Books-by-the Dozen. But no!

5 A storage shack or shed.

6 A city on Luzon island, located in a cool, mountainous region and known as the summer capital of the Philippines.

Tatay and *Nanay*[7] have to be at our farm in Batangas[8] to negotiate with some small businesses there to buy their local produce of fruits and vegetables. I am stuck with babysitting my impish brother for a month!

"You'll be okay, Cristina," *Nanay* reassures me. "Tita Neneng and Tito Boying[9] are just next door."

"Sure! Like they don't have enough kids to watch over," I whine.

"Tiya Tinay then," she replies.

I roll my eyes – *sure, like she'd be the more pleasant person to ask for help* – and bid my parents a cold goodbye.

So, here I am, stuck at home with the two people I'd rather avoid in my life right now.

* * *

I am still on my way back to our house, careful not to scrunch on the gravelled walk from Auntie's house for fear that she may hear me. No sooner does Jun-jun enter our house when I hear a sickening crash of glass and metal followed by the sound of a bouncing ball.

"Jun-jun! *Ano ba 'yan?*" (What is that?)

I rush through our front door to find shards of *Nanay*'s glass shelves, the shelves for her precious ceramic vase collection, scattered on the living room floor. And her vases, oh her vases, all in pieces.

"Jun-jun! *Ano ba 'yan!*" I yell at him. "This isn't a basketball court! Look at that!"

My brother's face turns as pale as paper. His lips are trembling. "Sorry, Ate Cris,"[10] he manages to say. But I don't care, I'm fuming mad.

7 Mother in Tagalog.
8 A province in Luzon known for its beaches and rolling terrain suitable for farming.
9 "Tito" means uncle in Tagalog.
10 "Ate" means older sister in Tagalog.

"Get out of here! Go to your room! It's only been a few hours with me stuck with you and already … this!"

I hear my brother's bedroom door close. Not slam. Just close.

Broken pieces of glass crunch under my feet. Good thing that I'm wearing those hard rubber flip-flops. I "angry-stomp" my way to the kitchen to fetch the broom and dustpan. Sweep, sweep, sweep. I use the dustpan like a shovel for the bigger shards of glass. Sweep some more. I "angry-stomp" my way to the large garbage bin just outside the backdoor of the kitchen and dump the pieces of glass into the bin, then go back into the house. I pick up Jun-jun's stupid basketball from the corner of the room, go back to the garbage bin and toss it in, too. *There! Let's see if you can find it now.*

I'm feeling feverish with anger, so I pour myself a glass of *calamansi*[11] juice and gulp it down. I pour myself another glass, finishing what's left in the pitcher. *There! See if I care that there isn't any left for you.*

Now, I'm tired from "angry-sweeping" the floor. I go to my room and switch on my laptop. *Hmm, who's on Facebook at this time of day?*

I'm just about to scroll down my Facebook feed when the doorbell rings. *Now what?*

"Jun-jun, stop it! I know it's you."

Nobody rings the doorbell of this house. The only doorbell needed is the one at the gate and it's connected to the front house because they're the closest at the front for opening the gate. Our doorbell is just for … nothing, really.

Again, the doorbell rings. *Ano ba!* (What now!)

"Jun-jun, I said stop it!" I yell from my room.

"Cristina!"

11 A small, very sour hybrid citrus fruit that looks like a small, round lime, commonly used in Filipino and Southeast Asian dishes and beverages.

Oh no, it's Tiya Tinay!

I rush out to unlock our front door. Then I remember that we don't lock our door because we're in a compound. I forget that there is only one person in this compound who unnecessarily rings the doorbell – Tiya Tinay.

"Cristina! What took you so long to open the door … plus shouting from your room … and what has Jun-jun done?"

"I was just … I'm sorry, didn't mean to … You heard?"

How on earth does Tiya Tinay know that something has happened here? And, why doesn't she just enter? She knows the door is unlocked.

"Heard what?"

"Oh! Uh, nothing. Ah, I thought that's why you came."

"Hmph."

Tiya Tinay holds up a bowl of potato salad in one hand. "I came to give you this. I wasn't sure if you had any lunch prepared or if you know how to make lunch. Or if your *Nanay* even cooked you some meals before leaving."

She knows pretty well that I can make a triple-decker sandwich for lunch, and that *Nanay* doesn't know how to cook either; it's *Tatay* who does the cooking in this house.

I reach out to take the bowl. Instead, she reaches out her other hand to me. I forget that she still expects us to practice the traditional greeting of taking an elder's hand and touching it to our forehead as a sign of greeting and respect.

"*Mano po, Tiya,*" I manage to mumble. "Thanks. We're okay here."

"Okay means barely passing. Barely eating. The salad is freshly made. It's the quickest I could make for you. There's enough time to chill it before lunch. Later, I will cook a better meal. Hot. For your supper. You should eat a proper meal in this house. And, where is your brother?"

"He's in his room."

"Still in bed at this time? Just because it's vacation time, it's not healthy to oversleep. Or did he oversleep because he slept very late last night?"

Breathe deeply. Breathe. She's leaving soon.

"Maybe I should wake him up," says Tiya Tinay.

I step back suddenly to make for Jun-jun's door. "I'll do it."

Tiya Tinay takes back the bowl of potato salad from me. "Meanwhile, into the refrigerator, this one," she says.

* * *

I knock on my brother's door. "Jun … Jun …" I whisper. "Come out now. It's *Tiya*. She's asking for you."

"I can't," he answers.

"Now, Jun! Out, now!"

"I can't."

"You can't or you won't," I say, as I push his door open.

Jun-jun is lying down on the floor with his right leg raised on the bed. Blood is trickling from a wound on his shin. A small piece of glass is sticking out of the cut.

"Jun-jun! Why didn't you call me?"

"You were mad. I'm sorry. I wanted to pull out the glass but … you know I can't stand the sight of blood. So I raised my leg up to stop the bleeding, just like they say on TV."

"Oh, Jun. You should have told me. Let's …"

"What is this? Huh, is that blood?" I hear Tiya Tinay's voice behind me.

Jun-jun immediately sits up to look like nothing's the matter. I am sent out of the room to fetch Tiya Tinay's first aid kit from the top drawer of the china cabinet in her dining room. Meanwhile, Tiya Tinay takes over the situation.

* * *

After Jun-jun's wound is cleaned and bandaged, Tiya Tinay insists on having lunch with us, just to make sure. *To make sure of what?* Neither Jun-jun nor I know. But we are just too tense at her presence to ask.

After eating, Tiya Tinay stands up to take her leave.

"I don't wish to be impolite but I have to go back home to do some chores."

My brother and I look at each other knowingly. We can almost read each other's minds. She's going to pick out the stones again.

"Cristina, after you're done doing the dishes here, I want to have a word with you. And you, Jun-jun, if you want that cut to heal fast, you have to take a *siesta*.[12] It will do you good. Cristina, he's your responsibility. You're his Ate Cris, so act like one. Your brother could have been hurt more seriously."

I resent her words. I'm always a responsible older sister, even when I don't feel like it. Besides, Jun is old enough to know not to bounce a ball near a glass shelf. It was just those few seconds when he was out of my sight that the accident happened. And, I cleaned up the mess immediately. I could've made our own lunch. I could've cleaned the wound myself. She just didn't give me the chance – just assumed I was no good.

I want to explain myself but Tiya Tinay turns her back to me and walks out the front door.

I do the dishes grudgingly at first until I realise that the water running over my hands helps to calm me down. *Next time, I'll speak up.*

* * *

Jun-jun sheepishly waits for me in the living room. He's seated on the sofa looking around in disbelief at how all evidence of his disaster has been swept clean. The only remaining proof are the empty metal brackets that used to hold the glass shelves.

12 Afternoon nap.

"You can take a nap on the sofa. It's cooler here than in your room," I say.

He obediently lies down flat on his back and stares at the ceiling.

"I'm sorry she scolded you instead of me," he says.

"Yah," is all I can mutter.

* * *

I take slow steps to the *bodega* house, thinking how aptly we nicknamed Tiya Tinay's house. *Bodega.* Storage house. She should just remain there and mind her own business. She's just a grumpy, old lady who is out of sync with the times. Strict and old-fashioned. A stickler for ancient rules of etiquette. A kill-joy.

I remember how she would often scold my younger cousins whenever they played hide-and-seek in our yard. They're kids, for heaven's sake! Who cares about ruining her hibiscus and *sampaguita* plants. They were growing wild around the place anyway. And what about that time my friends and I were singing karaoke in our living room – *our* living room! She showed up and told us to lower the volume of the music, not because we were out of tune, but because she had to go to bed by 7 o'clock in the evening. Then, there was Jun-jun, who couldn't play basketball without bouncing the ball. Too much noise, she'd say. Also, when *Nanay* tried baking her a birthday cake – she just took a tiny slice, saying it was bad for her blood sugar when she wasn't even diabetic.

Nothing really pleases her. There's always something to criticise. Always something that needs to be done or should not have been done. A real kill-joy.

* * *

I'm at her front door. *I can do this.* I enter the house.

Tiya Tinay is at the dining table, as expected. It's after lunch. The dishes are done. Time to bring out the rice container and her trusty *bilao*.[13] What a life. She does this every single day. At mid-morning and in the afternoon, each day, every day.

"Oh! You startled me. Didn't you knock first?" She knits her brows at me.

"But weren't you expecting me? You asked me to come after …"

"A polite visitor, whether a relative or not, always knocks first," she says.

Okay, now I don't feel like saying sorry. *I wasn't visiting. YOU asked me to come!*

"You aren't a child anymore. You should know these things. What will other people say about you being impolite? That perhaps your parents didn't raise you well. And, your duties as the older child – by now, you should be able to take care of your brother."

Her words are buzzing in my ear. *My brother is a normal 11-year-old. He's not retarded.* I feel a warmth creeping up my neck. My temples are throbbing. *Enough! Enough, you nagging old witch!*

"Are you done, *Tiya*?" I blurt out. It's too late now. The dam has burst. She glares at me. I glare back. "Because if you're done then I must go back to my brother and make sure he's safe and sound. Or is there something else you'd like to criticise about me?"

Tiya Tinay takes a deep breath and exhales through her mouth. I can feel silent, scolding words,ready to be blown out of that mouth and float towards me. She looks down at the grains of rice she was picking at. "Go," is all she says.

I hesitate to leave. Now is the time. I, myself, have so much to complain and rant about her.

"Why are you such a nagger, *Tiya*? You complain about the kids if they're noisy playing outside. But you also complain if

13 A flat, round woven basket tray for sorting out raw rice grains from stray seeds and small stones.

they're quietly lazing around the house. They're just kids. You criticise *Nanay* for not cooking, and you criticise *Tatay* for doing the cooking. You don't consider that *Nanay* does the laundry and ironing aside from her work in the office. And me? I stay out of your way to avoid displeasing you but you still seek me out just to find fault with me. You're just a sorry old spinster who has nothing better to do in life than to criticise and complain about others. Stick to picking out those stones in the rice. It's the only good thing you do. It will make everyone else here feel better."

Tiya Tinay stoically continues to sort out the rice grains. She does not look up to glare at me nor scold me for my impertinence.

There! You see? I have a voice, too.

I leave without looking back. The dam has burst. She just got washed away.

* * *

The rest of the day and over the next couple of days, Jun-jun and I live together in peace.

He's being extra nice to me for the trouble he has caused. Whatever house chores I ask him to help me with, he does so readily. He doesn't even yell at me when he finds his ball in the garbage bin. Babysitting this big baby isn't so bad, after all.

On Friday, Tito Boying drops by to leave us some groceries and food supplies for the next few days. Normally, I'd greet him with a wide smile. Today, however, there is no smile from me.

"Sorry for the short notice, Cristinay," he says. I wince at his pet name for me.

"Don't call me that, *Tito.*" I frown. It has always been his playful way of calling me since I was named after Tiya Cristina, better known as Tiya Tinay. I usually don't mind it, but not today.

"Why the grumpy face?"

"Nothing."

Tito Boying shrugs. "Your Tita Neneng and I are bringing the boys to Baguio for the weekend. We promised them this trip to start the summer right."

He clicks his tongue thrice and shakes his head in a half-joking way of imitating Tiya Tinay's probable reaction. This makes me smile.

"Now there's my Cristinay," he gently teases. I don't mind, this time.

I like Tito Boying. He has also been a constant target of Tiya Tinay's petty displeasure ever since he started courting Tita Neneng, and until now when they're married with six children.

"Don't let her get to you. She's really a darling deep down inside. She's awkward at accepting help, and even more awkward at giving help just to make her feel needed," he says and winks at me. "I was just at her place to leave her some supplies. She pretended to be annoyed at the favour I did for her but accepted them just the same. She cares. Even handed me some leftover bread pudding that she loves to make."

I smile weakly and bid Tito Boying a safe trip. Jun-jun is giving his cousins high-fives.

"Don't forget to bring my souvenirs," he says. "Bring me the famous Baguio strawberries and *ube*[14] jam."

The compound is suddenly quiet without Tito Boying's family. It's our responsibility now to check on the gate when we hear the doorbell ring. Thankfully, it's a buzzer that can be heard from our living room.

I think about what Tito Boying just said. *She offered him bread pudding even if she doesn't really like him. It's her awkward way of showing care?*

14 A purple yam called water yam or winged yam, commonly used in Filipino desserts.

Strangely, I feel my heart melt a bit. Just a bit. Then I shrug it off just to hold on to my anger at her.

* * *

Jun-jun and I are lazing around in the living room. I feel it is like an act of defiance. Just lazing around with no one to scold us.

"This feels weird," Jun-jun says.

"Weird? What's weird?"

Jun-jun sits up. "Weird. I half-expected *Tiya* to walk in and call us out."

I snicker. "She'd knock first. Or ring the doorbell."

"No, seriously," Jun-jun turns to me. "I haven't seen her come out in days to water her plants. Haven't even seen her at the dining table picking out rice stones as usual."

"Jun-jun! Have you been spying on her again?"

"Only once."

"*Ano ba!* You better stop it, na. It's not polite. Why can't you grow up and act your age?"

"I am acting my age. I'm only 11. Now you sound just like Tiya Tinay."

"Shut up, Jun-jun!"

"Just saying." He shrugs then stands up to go to his room.

Do I really sound like her? Will I end up as a grumpy, old maid like her? I can be grumpy at times but I'm also nice, otherwise. Can Tiya Tinay also be nice … otherwise?

Now I'm bothered. Something's eating at me. Was I too harsh? Did it cause her some heart attack? But Tito Boying didn't say anything was wrong.

My heart is racing. I don't know why. I just feel that I have to check on Tiya Tinay. Not to apologise, just to check on her. Yah, just to make sure she's okay.

* * *

I pause in front of her door, and raise my right fist. I knock on the door even if it's partially open.

No answer.

I knock again. Louder, this time.

Still no answer.

"Tiya Tinay? It's me." Silence.

Then, I hear a tapping from somewhere inside the house. *Heck!* I go in.

"*Tiya*?"

The bathroom door is open. The light is on.

"Cristina! I'm here!"

Her voice sounds like she's in pain and I rush in.

True enough, Tiya Tinay is sprawled on the bathroom floor. She's still fully clothed in her *daster*, the loose-fitting housedress she loves to wear, but she's soaked.

"I slipped," she says. "I was filling this pail so I could water my plants. I haven't watered them in days because my back pain has been acting up."

"Oh, *Tiya* ... don't move yet. We have to make sure there aren't any broken bones. I'll get a dry towel first."

I hurry to her bedroom and find a terry cloth robe hanging behind the door. *Perfect!*

In the bathroom, I wrap the robe around her shoulders and carefully slip off her wet housedress.

"It's not good for you to be soaked like this. You could catch a cold. Or worse, a cough. Even pneumonia. Next time, if the chore is too heavy, just ask for help." *Did I just scold her?*

She is shaking. I suppose more out of embarrassment at being seen naked than from the cold or pain. She doesn't seem to have any fractures as I gently feel her arms, back and legs.

"I'm fine," she says. "Just couldn't stand up by myself. Nothing broken. Except my ego, maybe."

Our eyes meet. I catch a twinkle in her eyes. And just like that, we're both laughing our hearts out, while still sitting on the bathroom floor.

"Aha ha ha … *ahay*!" She manages to sigh, and despite th stabbing pain, and settle down.

"Let me help you up then," I say.

Now, I feel a warmth flowing through my arms as I help Tiya Tinay stand and regain her balance. She hugs my waist and looks at my face again.

"You're too skinny," she playfully scolds me. "Let's both have some bread pudding I just made to fatten you up."

"Let's," I answer.

We both share an afternoon snack of bread pudding and cups of warm lemon tea. We forget to invite my brother. For now, it's just afternoon tea between two silly old maids. And that's okay.

Author's Note

The story is fiction but several details, when taken individually and separately, are true.

I grew up as an only child – something of a rarity for children of my generation. However, our small family was never without a visiting relative or family friend who would stay with us for a couple of days or, sometimes, an entire summer. I did have a spinster aunt (actually, I had two unmarried aunts) who spent her mornings and afternoons picking out the stones from our rice. She lived with us until she passed on. She did have her trusty *bilao*, that round, flat woven basket tray for winnowing rice grains. And, she loved to turn our days-old bread into buttermilk pudding.

Regarding the craft of writing, physical description is often used to introduce a character but the more technical aspect of writing that I paid attention to was the dialogue.

I wanted the readers to be immersed in each scene as they eavesdrop on the characters. Each character should sound appropriate for their personality. Tiya Tinay is formal and stern. Cristina is observant and emotionally eloquent, though funny, too. Jun-jun is, well, a younger brother. These variations in speech can be achieved through their sentence patterns and length, and even through word choices and verbal expressions. A nagging entails a long and uninterrupted speech. Submissiveness and doubt are felt through short utterances. Anger is expressed through a harsh choice of words. Even silence, or a character's refusal to speak, can reflect volumes about the person's emotional state.

Another element of fiction that I played around with is the setting. The family compound comprising three different yet related households mirrors the families that inhabit each home. The front house, being the closest to the gate, is lived in by a family that is more extroverted, loves to travel, and could very well be the life of the party in any family reunion. The middle house is resided by Cristina, who is caught in that in-between world of a teenager expected to take on more grown-up responsibilities but at the same time still has her youthful interests and desires. The back house is Tiya Tinay, the master of her own world with its rules and routines.

We can learn so much about a person through their speech and environment.

Anuara's Dream

Sohana Manzoor

In Bangladesh, most women of the working class are still illiterate or, at best, they have only very basic education. Women who work as household helpers are in particularly vulnerable positions. In many cases, they are single mothers who are abandoned by their husbands, and they work either full time or part time in the households. Few are able to save money from their earnings as they have little knowledge about banks. They usually leave their meagre savings with a male family member who often uses up their funds. So, it often happens that after working hard throughout their lives, these women end up destitute. Only a few lucky ones are helped by their former employers and are able to buy land in their villages.

Even though the government of Bangladesh has taken many steps to enhance women's education, in most rural families, women are married off at an early age (often as early as 14 or 15) if a suitable boy is found. The legal age for marriage for women is 18 and for men 21, but in rural areas, this rule does not apply. The government provides limited stipends for young girls to attend school and hence, many poor parents now send their daughters to school. These days, women also work and are expected to contribute extensively to their respective families. Yet, men are still considered the breadwinners even if they are not necessarily the major contributors.

Anuara sat in the warm winter sun in front of the tin-shed, three-room house she shared with her daughter. It had a separate toilet on one side of the yard. They had a kitchen at the other end of the yard which they shared with another family renting from the same landlord. People called her fortunate and extravagant because, after all, they did not really need three rooms, did they? Her daughter, Romela, and her husband could easily fit into one room while the children could share with her. But Anuara herself paid the rent of the extra room.

She reminded Romela every other day that she paid for one room and she should be grateful that she allowed her two grandchildren to sleep with her. Romela's husband, Dulal, owned a small roadside hotel[1] that sold rice, curry and other comestibles. The extra small room served as their dining and storage room. Romela helped her husband in preparing the food for sale. Sometimes they were quite comfortably off, but there were hard times too, especially during the rainy seasons when people had less work and there were fewer customers at Dulal's hotel. Anuara and Romela raised goats and chickens, and during those times, they often had to live on the animals. Dulal would grab a goat and sell it at the bazaar for 1,000 to 2,000 taka, depending on the size and gender of the animal. Anuara could not understand why a male goat would cost more than a female goat that could give birth to more goats. She made a face and thought how the world was unfair to females on all counts.

The small tin gate in front of their house opened and a boy of about ten entered with a yellow bag and a toothless grin. Anuara's creased and sour face cracked into a smile at the sight of her grandson, Abdul Aziz. "Baba Aziz, you're home early today! Where's your sister? Where's Tanjila?"

"Ma caught *Bubu*[2] on the way back and took her to the hotel to help with stuff," replied Aziz, while handing over his bag to his grandmother.

Immediately, Anuara's smile vanished. Her lips were pressed into a thin line and she asked, "And who will do the chores here?"

"Ma asked you to cook dal and rice. We have leftovers from yesterday."

1 In Bangladesh and India, a restaurant is often referred to as a hotel.
2 Older sister in Bangla.

Anuara's face darkened, "I don't live on her so that she can order me around. I have developed pain in the hips. I can't work and your mother knows that."

Abdul Aziz pouted before replying, "But I am hungry, *Nani*.[3] You won't feed your Azu?"

Anuara entered the kitchen grumbling. She sat before the clay oven and used husks to light it. If only they could live on the other side of town where there was a gas line, but then they would have to pay at least 1,000 taka more and with two school-going children. But they could not really afford it. Anuara washed the rice and put the pot with water and rice on the oven. If Dulal was more diligent, they could all live comfortably. But he was a lazy bum and had never been otherwise.

Measuring out two lentil varieties, Anuara put them together to cook dal. They had *shutki maach*[4] and some vegetable curry from the previous night, and this would be good enough for lunch. She grimaced as she got up; she was not lying about the pain in her hips. Romela often forgot that her mother was not the sturdy woman she was just a few years ago. But then children never remembered their parents; they only cared about their own little ones. Anuara, too, did everything she could for Romela. And now, as she was old and feeble, Romela merely tolerated her, and that too, Anuara suspected, was for the 6,000 taka that came from Dhaka every month.

Aziz's face lit up as he saw the boiled egg on his plate beside the rice and dal. He was not very fond of *shutki* and Anuara remembered that. She said dryly, "Eat your food before Tanjila comes back. I can't get another egg for her."

"You don't love *Bubu*," observed Aziz.

Anuara snorted.

3 Maternal grandmother in Bangla.
4 Dried fish in Bangla.

"But she's your grandchild, too."

"She cares more for the old witch who lives on the other side of the house. *She* can provide her with eggs. These are eggs from my chickens and I'll do as I please."

Anuara jealously guarded her chickens and eggs from Tanjila. It was true that Tanjila hovered around her paternal grandmother who lived with her eldest son in the adjacent house. When the old woman was seriously ill a few months ago, Tanjila used to wash her clothes. But she did not show the same concern for her maternal grandmother. Anuara was affronted and felt that she deserved more appreciation from her daughter's family than she received. But Aziz was a darling. He always showed affection and respect for his granny and often told her, "When I grow older, I'll look after you, *Nani*. Don't you worry!"

Anuara shrugged off his promises, but was pleased, too.

She watched as Aziz broke the egg and mashed it into his rice and dal with a pinch of salt. The bright yellow yolk mixed with dal produced a nice colour, and a familiar aroma wafted from it. Anuara asked tenderly, "Tastes good, Azu?"

Aziz smiled affectionately at his waspish grandmother whose only kind words were reserved for him. Anuara had stowed away a gold necklace, something she had bought from her wages while working in Dhaka. She had made a promise to give it to Aziz's wife when he got married. When she was in a good mood, she would take it out and allow Aziz to finger it. She also had some other trinkets that her kind mistress had given her. She had earned a lot but she was naïve in her younger days, and had left her money with her brother who basically used up all her funds. Even now, Anuara often cried over the lost fortune. The fact that her wastrel brother was bedridden and dying of liver disease did not abate her anger. A few days ago, his daughter had come to visit and Anuara cursed her, "Die, die all of you! What do you want from me? Get out!" She had picked up a broom and chased the poor girl out.

Nasima, her niece, ran out screaming and crying. Romela and the other neighbouring women had to restrain Anuara, who continued yelling, "That black sheep of the family! He cheated us of our father's property and ate up my money, too! What do I care if he's dying? Let him die like a dog! Let him rot in hell to his seventh generation! What's it to me?"

The only dream Anuara had now was to build a small house on the piece of land she had bought two years ago with her savings. She had already saved a bit but it would require at least 50,000 taka to build just two rooms and a bathroom. If only Dulal could earn a little more, she would have saved the money her former mistress sent every month as her pension, and the house would be built in no time. Instead, she had to share the money with her daughter for this and that. She could not save more than 2,000 every month.

"Aunty could surely send another 2,000," said Romela the other day when Anuara returned home with some sticks and rice husks for their clay oven.

Anuara knitted her brows and looked at her daughter. Romela said, "Then we could move to the other part of town where they have gas lines."

Anuara put her burden down and entered the kitchen without a word. Romela ploughed on, "Couldn't you ask Aunty? She sends only 6,000. With growing kids …"

Anuara cut her short. "She does not send the money for your kids. She sends that for me, for the service I rendered to her ailing mother. Don't forget that she sent money for Dulal, too, when he was at the hospital. He would not be alive today if she had not sent that 25,000." She paused and added, "I won't ask for more. She has given more than anybody has ever given me.

Tell me, would you have looked after me last winter if she had not sent money? She not only paid me during that time, but still keeps on sending money."

Romela's face went red. "Ma, you always find fault with me for not caring enough for you!"

"Do you? You care for the money, your kids and that good-for-nothing husband of yours. Where am I in the picture?"

Romela started to cry. "I don't earn, *Amma*,[5] and your son-in-law is not well off. Do you have to insult us all the time for the money you give us?"

Anuara looked up from her work and said, "Well, your in-laws insult me for staying with you. They even say I live on their son, when in reality you live on me. I also sell eggs and chickens. Two of the goats were bought with my money. I paid for that piece of land in your name. Why don't you people let me go and live on my own? Because you need my money. I have no illusion, Daughter. I lost it all years ago. My *apa*[6] in Dhaka is the only one who cares, and it's because of her that I have what I have, not because of any of you."

Romela's wailing subsided into sniffing. Every word her mother had uttered contained the bitter truth. It was not that she did not care for her mother, but the everyday needs plus two growing children along with a lazy husband drove her mad sometimes. What could she do? She had planned to work in people's houses sometime back. Her husband and mother-in-law had screamed their heads off. Her own mother had said nothing. She did not talk much these days unless they provoked her. Her mother's only heartfelt communication was with Aziz, and Romela felt a pang sometimes when she watched them from a distance. Once upon a time, she was very close to her mother, but somewhere along the road of life, the communication had stopped.

5 Mother in Bangla.
6 Sister or mistress in Bangla.

After an early dinner when Anuara was finishing her prayers, she heard howling and whimpering from the next room. She did not interfere. But then she heard Tanjila crying and Romela yelling at top of her voice, "Your *nani* pays your school fees. Azu's, too. If you cannot show her the minimum respect, and instead choose to listen to your *dadi*'s[7] lies, then go and ask her to pay for you! *Go!*"

Anuara froze. So, the old woman in the other house had started causing problems again. Was she so jealous of Anuara that she would try to throw her out of this house? And in such a devious way? She sighed. She got up and stepped out of her room. Outside, the evening was slowly turning into a dark night. The sky was moonless. Standing by the door of Romela's room, she called out, "Romu! Don't hit your daughter."

Tanjila rushed out of the room, hugged Anuara and sniffled, "*Nani*, Ma has slapped me so hard that my lips are bleeding!"

Romela was still trembling in anger, "If I ever hear such nonsense from you, Tanjila, I am going to leave this house along with my mother. Do you understand? Then you can all live with your *dadi* and see who feeds who."

Tanjila had never seen her mother so angry, and Anuara could feel her granddaughter trembling like a leaf. She cried in silence, burying her face in the shoulder of the grandmother she was slandering just a few minutes ago. She always felt that her *nani* loved Aziz more. Everybody loved Aziz more, even her other grandmother. What did Tanjila not do to please her? For a few affectionate words from her, Tanjila was conspiring against the *nani* who basically kept them fed, sheltered and clothed during hard times. She wept bitter tears but suddenly stopped as the words of her *nani* sank in. She was saying, "Don't beat up your daughter, Romu. If you hurt her like that, she might end up having blemishes. She is a girl and you have to get her married.

7 Paternal grandmother in Bangla.

And you know these are not her ideas. Your mother-in-law has been poisoning her."

Romela cried, "I'm just fed up. I do everything for their upkeep and if my own daughter doesn't understand, what can I do?" She paused and said, "She is 16 now, maybe we should just marry her off. Forget about sending her to school. I will have one less mouth to feed."

Tanjila's face went as white as a sheet. Her body went limp. Stop her education and get married? In no time, she would be with children and her life would become like her mother's. She wailed, "I want to study, Mother, don't do this to me!"

Anuara's hand went around her granddaughter and she said, "Of course, you will study. Your mother is just angry. Focus on studying. Don't listen to your *dadi*. You think of your exams."

When Tanjila went to bed that night, her brother whispered, "You're such a fool, *Bubu*. Why do you listen to the old woman in that house? She is jealous. Has she ever done anything for us?"

Tanjila did not say anything. She knew that her *nani* paid for their school, but she had always thought that she lived on them and paid for their education out of gratitude. She was still half-sure that her *dadi* was right. As she fell asleep, the last thought on her mind was to ask her father and Shefu Khala, who was her mother's best friend.

When Tanjila woke up the next morning, Anuara's side of the bed was empty as usual. She was always up before anyone else in the house. After saying her prayers, she would massage ointment on her sore hips. Then she would take the goats out to graze. This morning was no different, but when she did not return even after everybody had finished their breakfast, Romela was a bit surprised. "Where did *Amma* go? She's usually back by this time."

Anuara returned two hours later, after Tanjila and Azu went off to school. She had a look of resolution on her face. When

Romela asked where she had gone, Anuara did not reply. Romela let it go because she knew her mother would not say anything if she did not want to.

After supper that night, Anuara finally spoke. "I have decided to borrow from the co-op office. I have already spoken to them. I will borrow 1 lakh taka from the office to build a proper house on the piece of land."

Everybody gasped. Dulal opened his mouth first, "When did you talk to the co-op office people?"

"This morning. I have had enough of living here. I will have a house of my own. And since the land is in Romela's name, you can choose to live there, too. But I will have that house built. I am sick of hearing that I live on my daughter and her husband."

"How will you pay it off, *Amma*?" asked an awestruck Romela.

"I will sell my jewellery if necessary. And I will also ask *Apa* to give me some money. I think she will if I explain the situation."

Dulal said lamely, "How can I live in my wife's house?"

"Then go and live with your mother," replied an angry Romela. "I am sure she will treat you with rice and milk, allow you to sell her goat and perhaps marry you off to a rich widow."

Aziz sprang up, "That will be so great. And, you can then save on the rent money. Oh *Nani*, you are wonderful."

Tanjila said timidly, "Will you allow me to live there, too? That side of town is so green."

Anuara replied with a twinkle in her eyes, "Of course. We are a family and we live together."

Dulal looked at the hopeful and blooming faces of his wife and children. He knew he had failed them as a husband and father. He heaved a long sigh and said, "All right, we'll all go."

Anuara sat down to peel a bundle of green betel nuts. She loved the slightly intoxicating taste of the nuts. It would not be easy, she knew, to build the house. Dulal's family would cause a lot of problems. But she had to make it happen, to save her daughter and grandchildren from those greedy and jealous people. Also, they needed a home of their own to live in. After her death, Romela would inherit everything. She looked at the gangly shadow of Tanjila. The girl was too tall for a young woman. "Tanjila, come here," she called out. "Sit with me."

When Tanjila came and sat gingerly by her grandmother's side, Anuara gave her a few wet nuts to chop. She was quite deft at it. Anuara said in a soft voice, "I've decided I will give you my dangling gold earrings if you achieve good results in your exams."

Tanjila's fingers faltered just a little, and she turned to look at her grandmother who had always said that all her jewellery would go to Aziz's future wife. "B … but …" she started to speak. Anuara stopped her in mid-sentence and said, "Girls also deserve good things in life. Manage your studies properly – you'll see that life is good."

Romela watched them from a distance and a strange feeling started to grow in her chest. It was very small at first, and then it gave a little leap. It jumped and grew. Then it started spreading and Romela suddenly recognised what it was. It was happiness, a feeling of contentment that she thought had died many years ago.

Author's Note

I am not someone who learnt to write consciously. I told stories to my siblings and cousins as I was growing up. I picked up story elements, narratives and characters as I saw them around me – and I see stories around me all the time.

When I wrote "Anuara's Dream", my inspiration was an elderly woman called Anowara, who had worked for my family for many years and looked after my mother during her final days. In 2018, she left to live with her daughter and her family, and we have remained in touch. When she was living with us, she often told me about her life, the difficulties she had encountered and her dreams. I felt that hers was a story similar to many other women in her station in life. I thought of writing a story about her for quite some time. I did some secondary research in trying to understand her social situation and difficulties. I tried to appreciate and recreate the complexities of in-law relationships in the story.

While I used real-life scenarios, the story is nevertheless fictional. I used observational methods to understand the way working class people live, think and conduct themselves. The women have it the hardest, and as I have shown through Anuara and her daughter's family, the burden of raising children rests on women while men have an easier life and often take out their negative emotions on their women. It reflects how the women are subservient to the men in their families, and the men consider the women their property.

The story is a third-person narrative that focuses mainly on Anuara and how she looks on her past life as a domestic helper. In spite of her early struggles from being abandoned by her husband and family, she was able to carve out a place for herself. However, she has one last dream for herself and her daughter, whom she loves very much but is not able to vocalise it. The angle of the narration shifts at the end from Anuara to her daughter, as it does once in a while throughout the story. This was done to show how the central character appears to others around her. Her stern, eccentric and taciturn behaviour is reflective of the hardship and betrayals she had faced in her life.

The Scarlet Kanjivaram

Sumitra Selvaraj

The saree is a single length of unstitched fabric, typically between six to nine yards in length. The garment is worn as a skirt-like drape around the lower body with one end slung over the shoulder. The different styles in which a saree is draped over the body originate from the different regions in India. The saree traces its roots back to the days of the Indus Valley Civilisation, and with a history of over 6,000 years, it is one of the world's oldest garments in form and function.

Although the saree is a gender-fluid item of clothing, it is predominantly worn by women of the Indian subcontinent and diaspora. Sarees are highly utilitarian and are worn as everyday attire by millions of women in India. Younger generations may choose western attire over the saree, but it is still seen as a vital cultural element to mark rites of passage, such as marriage rituals.

The more expensive sarees are handwoven from pure silk and may contain varying degrees of real gold thread and other costly embellishments. The undisputed queen of wedding sarees is the Kanjivaram saree produced in the temple city of Kanchipuram in Tamil Nadu, India. It is crafted with such a high degree of skill that it has been accorded a Geographical Indication Tag by the Indian Government. Authentic Kanjivaram sarees are considered heirlooms to be passed down through the generations.

Scarlet Kanjivaram came to life as her final threads were woven into place. She stretched her six-yard long form, straining ever so slightly as she was still attached to the loom. As the weaver snipped the bindings tethering her to the wooden frame which had birthed her, the saree felt for the first time the lush weight of her own being.

She was lifted off the handloom by two men and taken

to an adjoining room. She was laid on the clean cement floor, examined and neatly folded before she even had time to take in her surroundings. Tucked on a shelf with others, Kanjivaram cautiously sniffed the earthy scent of her silken saree sisters.

Hours and days passed, before the woman with a rosebud smile reached up to take her off the shelf. Scarlet Kanjivaram sensed that something exciting was about to happen. Unfolded and displayed, she heard the weaver sing her praises as his calloused hands gently ran over her body, pointing out the exquisite details. She knew from the way the woman's fingers traced the gold thread motifs that she was about to leave the weaver forever, just as she had seen others depart the home they briefly shared. She would miss the weaver, of course, so she considered leaving a thread behind for him to remember her by. It would not be too difficult to try and snag herself against a corner of the table, but she decided that it might end up hurting her chances of leaving, so instead she threw him a shimmer that she hoped looked like gratitude, before sliding into a jute bag.

Scarlet Kanjivaram knew her purpose, how could she not, when it was all the other sarees on the shelf could talk about. They were all special sarees, she was told – grand, occasion-wear sarees meant to be draped for the most significant events in a woman's life. And so Scarlet Kanjivaram was a little confused when she discovered that the woman with the rosebud mouth, who was called Pavithra, showed no indication of wanting to wear her. Their first day together was uneventful to say the least; after travelling for what felt like hours, Scarlet Kanjivaram emerged from the jute bag only to be laid out on a bed in a room where the air hummed in a different way from the fan-cooled air of the weaver's home. She watched Pavithra empty bag after bag onto the bed until there was a pile of sarees that Scarlet Kanjivaram recognised as all her own kind.

"We're going to Malaysia," said Sapphire Blue, in a tone that made every other Kanjivaram want to trust her.

"I know, because this Pavithra woman comes every few months to my weaver and picks a few to travel with her."

"But there are so many of us," exclaimed Turmeric.

"How many Kanjivarams does she really need?"

"Why do you have so little gold thread on you?" shot back Lotus Pink which was adorned with beady-eyed peacocks.

Scarlet Kanjivaram bristled on hearing that last question, even though it had not been directed at her. "Not all Kanjivaram sarees need a profusion of gold," she said pointedly to Lotus, whose peacocks glared at her for coming to Turmeric's defence.

"Easy for you to say," sniffed Lotus. "You are a red saree."

In the days that followed, Scarlet Kanjivaram often thought about that comment made by Lotus. She knew red was an auspicious colour; she had heard the weaver say it numerous times to his assistants and to the customers who occasionally visited his work area to inspect his sarees. She knew she was special; the other Kanjivarams she had sat on a shelf with had inferred that she was lucky to be born a red saree. But she did not quite understand what it all added up to. She was not the most elaborate saree, not by far. Most of her shelf sisters and certainly all her companions in the room that they now knew was in a hotel, had far more gold thread on them. Well, all except Turmeric, whose simple nature matched the lack of embellishment on her body. Scarlet Kanjivaram had taken an instant shine to Turmeric's open and friendly manner, and they quickly developed a friendship. It was from Turmeric that Scarlet Kanjivaram learned that the motifs on her own body were unique; while peacocks and elephants were common enough as were floral vines as on Turmeric's borders, Scarlet Kanjivaram was festooned with gold threadwork horses that galloped along her length.

"Quite like a circus, isn't it? Or am I thinking of a zoo?" remarked Lotus, who drew her silver threadwork peacocks closer around her.

"Don't mind that one, Scarlet," said Turmeric quietly.

"The Pinks can be nasty pieces of work."

* * *

A rush of air woke Scarlet Kanjivaram from her slumber – she felt like she had been buried for days. Strong lights pierced her fogginess and then flooded her senses as she was snatched up and brought into an unfamiliar room.

"Hey! Careful, please," she heard Pavithra say as she was placed on a counter which afforded her a full view of the space she had emerged from. It was certainly no longer the hotel room as sunshine streamed in through glass windows that looked out onto a view of a busy street.

This must be Malaysia, thought the Scarlet Kanjivaram excitedly. The room was lined with wooden shelves from floor to ceiling and she was surrounded by hundreds of Kanjivaram sarees in every shade imaginable. There were familiar reds and blues and greens, and some colours that she had never seen before. Those jewelled tones seemed to dance in the light even while lying still. For the first time, she saw more red sarees than she, ever thought possible. The reds took up an entire wall of shelves; stacked vertically and exposing just a hint of their embellishments. With shimmering brocade work, intricate motifs and hues ranging from brick to burgundy, the red sarees dominated the colour palate in the room. Scarlet Kanjivaram was suddenly aware of her plainness – even her rambunctious horses whom she loved dearly suddenly seemed out of place in this elegant environment. She took her place on a low shelf next to a checked Chilli and was thankful that at least the yellows were within sight on an adjacent wall. She noticed that Turmeric's companions were cheerily welcoming her to the fold, and she was happy for her friend, despite missing her reassuring company.

In the weeks and months that followed, Scarlet Kanjivaram keenly observed the comings and goings of Pavithra's saree store. She found the customers fascinating and played a little game with herself to try and guess which colour saree they would be attracted to even before they approached the counter. She learned to recognise the many different types of brides: happy, shy, stressed, and once, just once, a girl whose reluctance was clutched in a clenched fist. Some of the women who were looking for a wedding saree were accompanied by whole entourages, others strolled in, hand in hand with their partners. Some entered the store with their doting parents, while others had the delightful company of their friends as they browsed for sarees to complete their trousseau. None of the brides came alone.

Pavithra would ask each and every woman directly what they wanted in a saree, but the answer did not always come from them. Scarlet Kanjivaram concluded that the larger the entourage accompanying a woman, the less likely the bride would leave with her choice of saree. This was especially true if they were family members accompanying the woman. She watched one bride's eyes light up when Turquoise was placed before her, only to have it shoved aside by a bony hand which snapped its fingers and demanded to see something better. The excitement that another young woman felt when she spied Aubergine was palpable as she squealed in delight, but it never made it off the shelf of purples as her father ordered her to select a different saree.

Let her have what she wants, screamed Scarlet Kanjivaram, but of course no one paid her any heed. In fact, no one even wanted to look at her as soon as they heard that she did not have traditional woven borders and her motifs were horses.

"What a shame for such a pretty colour," said one shopper disdainfully.

"Is it just an office wear saree?" enquired another.

"If there is some flaw in it, then is there a discount by any chance?" This was another popular query about Scarlet Kanjivaram.

Pavithra would patiently explain that there was nothing wrong with a borderless saree; yes, it was a little less elaborate than most Kanjivaram sarees, but the spectacular details of the equine motifs made it quite a unique piece of art.

"Horses, though," would come the puzzled response.

"Are you sure those are not cows?"

I'll show you a cow, thought Scarlet Kanjivaram as she was returned to her spot on the shelf.

* * *

The woman who walked into the store on an overcast afternoon was draped in an ivory linen saree over a black sleeveless blouse. The only jewellery she wore was a pair of silver hoops in her ears and anklets which tinkled along with the bell at the threshold. She carried a long black umbrella, tightly furled and with a carved handle, which was old-fashioned and quirky. But the umbrella did not look like it would really be much use against the torrential rain that the last month had brought.

And yet Scarlet Kanjivaram instantly fell in love with her for carrying it, for the ease in which her saree was slung over her shoulder, and for her wide grin as she took in the kaleidoscope of sarees around her. The woman also had a dark leather handbag which she removed from the crook of her arm and threw onto the floor before enveloping Pavithra in a warm embrace.

There was not a single Kanjivaram in the store which could contain their curiosity. It was rare enough for someone to walk into the store dressed in a saree, but this woman was not even paying any of them an inch of attention, besides her cursory glance round the store when she entered. And yet, she was clearly looking for a special saree, as it was the first thing they heard her announce, after the two women had hugged.

It took a good ten minutes of chatting and speculating before most of the Kanjivarams lost interest and settled down, but Scarlet Kanjivaram was on the edge of her shelf.

"It is going to be me today," she said slowly.

"What do you mean," snapped Strawberry who was trying to arrange herself to show off her gilded parrot motifs.

Scarlet Kanjivaram ignored the question and willed the woman to turn towards her.

Pavithra rose from her chair and said, "I have exactly what you're looking for."

Scarlet Kanjivaram watched as beaming Turmeric was brought down from her shelf and presented to the woman.

"Perfect," she laughed. "Absolutely perfect on the first go, Pavithra."

"Are you sure?" asked Pavithra, grinning at her friend's delight. "You know, Seema, brides do not usually buy the first saree that they pick off the shelf."

"Well, lucky for you, Pavithra, I'm not your usual bride!" twinkled the woman, holding Turmeric against her shoulder and inspecting her reflection in a mirror.

"No, you are most certainly not," agreed Pavithra, moving to refold Turmeric whose emanating joy threatened to blow out every lighting fixture in the store.

Scarlet Kanjivaram felt an unfamiliar emotion. It was not disappointment; no, she recognised and had dealt with that before. This was something else.

I am not wanted, thought Scarlet Kanjivaram as she sank back on her shelf.

Despite the feeling, Scarlet Kanjivaram admonished herself. *Be happy for the happiness of others*, she told herself firmly, even though the words tasted like frog skin. She hugged herself tightly, digging deep to conjure up a wave of warm wishes to send towards her friend.

You can do it, and Turmeric deserves this, she thought, and just as she did, she felt herself being lifted and carefully unfolded.

"And ... I was thinking of this, for the main event," said Pavithra.

"Horses," smiled Seema, "and in my favourite colour too. You, my lovely one, are exactly what I want to wear for my wedding," she said, gathering Scarlet Kanjivaram in her arms.

* * *

"And that's why even after being aired for two days, I still smell of chicken curry," said Lavender Cotton to hoots of laughter from the other sarees in the wardrobe.

"But wait, are you not going to tell us what happened when you were being aired out?" inquired Paisley Printed Silk. And to a chorus of encouragement, Lavender Cotton continued regaling her saree sisters with her adventures.

Scarlet Kanjivaram listened with quiet pride from the back of the wardrobe. Story time had been her idea when she arrived at the wardrobe two years ago. The other sarees had regarded her and Turmeric with a fair bit of suspicion. But, you could not blame them as they had never met a Kanjivaram before, let alone two at the same time. Scarlet Kanjivaram saw the other sarees eyeing her gold threadwork and heard their whispers about the richness of her fabric – right there and then, she decided to do something to break the ice.

Instead of waiting for others to approach her, she asked the sarees if they would mind if she shared what she and Turmeric had experienced over the last week. She asked Turmeric to describe the gaiety of the engagement party and how the music and colours were so intoxicating. The other sarees moved closer as Turmeric painted a vivid scene: a white canopy festooned with fairy lights, and a laughing Seema having her hands painted with henna while Arjun fed her bites of food. Turmeric showed them where a small henna stain now graced her body as a memory of that night, and the other sarees sighed at the keepsake. And then slowly, they turned to Scarlet Kanjivaram as she explained the intricacies of the wedding ceremony that she had participated in, and how she felt the purest joy radiate from Seema as she nestled up to Arjun on the decorated dais. As the other sarees gathered even closer, they could smell the faint scent of incense that still permeated Scarlet Kanjivaram despite having been dry-cleaned. They listened to her describe the heat of the sacred fire which had snaked closer than she would have liked and how the crescendo of drums was so deafening that she could not make out the words Arjun whispered in Seema's ear as he tied the thali around her neck. Without leaving out a single moment, Scarlet Kanjivaram recounted the day in such exquisite detail until Pistachio Cotton Silk remarked that she felt like she had been at a wedding too. The others murmured in agreement.

It was then that the Scarlet Kanjivaram suggested that other sarees returning to the wardrobe could share their stories, too, so that everyone would have a little insight into the events in Seema's life. The idea was received with much enthusiasm and, very quickly, story time became a tradition that all of them looked forward to.

Seema wore sarees regularly in those first two years, so there was always a new adventure to be shared. The sarees who returned told tales of parties and picnics, visiting friends and family, the movies and plays they had watched as well as the art galleries and museums that they had wandered through. The sarees that were lucky enough to travel told tales of their trips through lands where people spoke different languages, and once of what it felt like to be on the deck of an enormous vessel in the middle of a crystal blue sea. Sunset Cotton Silk described returning to the home of her weaver and how he had clapped his hands in delight at seeing his creation visit him. This story was met with envy for it was this journey to India that all the sarees coveted most of all. Occasionally, one of them would develop a tear, and return from the tailor with quite indignant accounts of being darned and mended. Only once did a saree disappear. Batik Silk whose colour had bled thanks to an unfortunate episode at the laundrette and was taken away despite her tear-stained protests. But Lavender Cotton returned one day from walking the dog and said that she was sure that she had seen fragments of Batik Silk sewed into small cushion covers. This then triggered an intense discussion amongst the sarees about whether it was better to be thrown away, or cut up and repurposed. After much deliberation, the consensus was that it was better to live on in a different form rather than being discarded forever.

Scarlet Kanjivaram listened to stories after every outing, and often wondered when her turn would come. She had not left the wardrobe since returning from the wedding and while she accepted that perhaps she was a more elaborate saree than the cottons and light silks that could be worn often, surely she was fit for a dinner party or two?

"Perhaps Seema is saving you for a special occasion," suggested Turmeric kindly.

"Perhaps," said Scarlet Kanjivaram, wondering when that would be.

* * *

One evening, Turmeric returned from the wedding of one of Seema and Arjun's friends, barely able to contain her glee. She had overheard a conversation between two women who had sat behind her and they had been talking about the bride's unusually heavy and ornate Kanjivaram. Wading through the snide comments and prickly observations, Turmeric had gleaned an important piece of information. She knew when Scarlet Kanjivaram was going to be worn next! Apparently, the wedding Kanjivaram was often worn when a woman was in her seventh month of pregnancy for a ceremony to celebrate the mother and baby's good health.

"Is Seema pregnant?" the others asked excitedly.

Turmeric did not think so, but the snippet of information was enough to send the sarees into quite a flurry of excitement.

"Maybe I'll get to be a swaddling cloth and hug the baby all day long," said soft White Muslin, already imagining what baby-powder-scented play time would feel like.

"Better hope you don't end up as diapers," giggled Charcoal Linen as the Muslin glowered at her.

"What are you doing?" asked Turmeric as she saw sturdy Brown Cotton inspecting herself.

"Oh, I'm just checking for signs of weakness. I'm hoping that I'll get to be a cradle, you know like the sling type babies can nap in."

"You must all realise that there isn't even a baby yet," said Scarlet Kanjivaram, doing her best to keep her own enthusiasm in check.

"Not yet," said Turmeric, "but we shall wait and see, of course!"

And so, the sarees waited patiently for little signs that Seema and Arjun were expecting a child, but after every outing they always returned to the wardrobe trying to hide their own disappointment from Scarlet Kanjivaram.

However, something else did happen. The sarees soon realised that they were being used less and less, until one of them pointed out that it had been months, or maybe even a year, since Seema had worn a saree. The wardrobe door remained resolutely shut, until the sarees themselves lost track of time.

* * *

Scarlet Kanjivaram had been dreaming of Seema's wedding day, when a sliver of light split the ink of the wardrobe. A pair of unfamiliar hands started to riffle through the sarees, a little too roughly, most of them thought. The hands were brusque, unlike Seema's which would often caress a saree or straighten a fold as she decided on what to wear. It was clear that these hands were on a mission as Scarlet Kanjivaram was dragged forward and she felt a rising panic.

Perhaps this is it, whispered Turmeric. But when Scarlet Kanjivaram glanced back at her friend, she too felt the uncertainty of the other sarees she left behind as the wardrobe door slammed shut.

Something was very wrong.

A stranger gripped Scarlet Kanjivaram in a rough bunched- up way, and off they went down the stairs. The air smelled oddly familiar, and then realisation struck.

There is a wedding in the house, thought Scarlet Kanjivaram.

The flowers and incense mingled to create a heavy atmosphere but there was another anxious element that Scarlet Kanjivaram could not recognise. She wanted nothing more than to be back in the safety of the wardrobe with her sisters.

She heard Arjun's voice say, "yes, that is the one," but it was not really his voice, not as she remembered it. It sounded dense, like it had grown tendrils in his throat and was now choking him.

They entered a room and Scarlet Kanjivaram felt every emotion being drained straight out of her silken fibres.

Seema was lying on a bed with her eyes closed and her hands clasped across her chest over a sheet that lightly covered her. Scarlet Kanjivaram heard quiet, snuffling sobs and whispers of words that meant nothing to her. She was placed on a chair and a bustle of activity obscured Seema's form from her.

A woman whom she remembered from Seema's wedding picked her up and held her a little more tenderly than the woman before. She smoothed the creases on the bright red silk and began gently pleating Scarlet Kanjivaram up.

"Such a thing of beauty you are," whispered the woman sadly.

"Please ask your golden horses to keep our darling Seema company as she journeys on," said the woman quietly, as Scarlet Kanjivaram was laid against Seema's skin that no longer pulsed with the warmth and radiance she had once fallen in love with at first sight.

Author's Note

As a regular saree wearer, I spend a couple of minutes every day thinking about what I have chosen to wear and how the saree came to be in my possession. Most of my sarees are hand-me-downs from my grandmother and mother; many others are gifts from loved ones. Every single saree has a story. For almost five years now, I have been documenting my daily drape on social media by sharing not just information about the type and style of saree that I wear but also the associated memories. Along the way, I found myself assigning personalities to many of my sarees and started writing vignettes of imaginary conversations that the sarees might have between themselves. "The Scarlet Kanjivaram" was written from this perspective: a saree's journey as experienced from its creation to life with its owner.

In writing the story, I thought about my own wedding saree and tried to recall the scene at the store where my husband-to-be and I had purchased my bridal drape. It occurred to me that I had no memories of anything else that day, except selecting my saree. There would have been sarees that we considered and rejected, of course. So this was an emotion that I wanted to explore from the perspective of the sarees that did not make the cut. I also wanted the story to show how sarees can be everyday attire, and not just worn for special events.

The scenes in Seema's wardrobe of the camaraderie between the sarees were the easiest to write because I had already imagined my own sarees having all kinds of cupboard confessionals. I tried to give different sarees distinct characters by having them experience various facets of Seema's life, but in the earlier sections had the sarees adopt the familiar dynamics that you might see in a social group. Attributing these personality traits of jealousy, kindness and being timid, helped me look at the various sarees as being self-aware and made it easier to flesh out the characters. I also wanted the central character, Scarlet Kanjivaram, to experience growing up through the story, by moving from being part of a group of sarees to taking on a leadership role.

The March

Tina Jimin Walton

In 1945, after World War II, an arbitrary line on the 38th parallel divided a once unified nation, Korea. The split in political ideologies forced upon Korea by geopolitical powers led to this division and shortly after, the Republic of Korea in the south and the Democratic People's Republic of Korea in the north were formed.

On 25 June 1950, communist North Korea, supported by the Soviets, declared the "liberation" of South Korea from western capitalism and started the Korean War. The surprise invasion rapidly captured Seoul and nearly all of the rest of the South. Many South Koreans were fearful of the "Reds", as North Koreans were called. They fled their homes in haste, taking whatever possessions they could on their backs, and walked for miles and miles further south in search of refuge. Hunger was a persistent companion, and families were separated in the wartime chaos. Children were forced to grow up quickly as they had to adapt to wartime conditions to survive. Eventually, UN troops, led by the Americans, pushed back the North Korean army, but any encounter with soldiers, UN, North or South, brought fear and confusion to many citizens.

It was the birds that eventually saved them, leading them off the bare mountain side and into the oasis of a small village. For weeks they had blindly followed a trail of refugees that streamed out of the capital shortly after the North Koreans invaded Seoul. Hong's older brothers were daring, staying behind at the university campus, posing as student socialists. But there was no faking for their father, a landowner. It would only be a matter of time before the communists combed through the records and found their father's ties with the capitalist officials.

He'd be finished.

Hong wanted to stay on with his brothers, but they quickly dismissed him, mussing his hair. "You're too young. Go with our parents," they had said. "You can't help anyway." Hong's brothers stayed on to keep an eye out for their home because they were certain the UN-backed army would eventually recapture Seoul.

Hong and his parents left in haste. They wore clothes on top of clothes, lined with inner seams that hid their money. Hong's mother was saddled with the biggest bundle, carrying their worldly possessions on her back, while Hong bore the heavy sack of rice. They didn't know where they were going – just south. They relied on the exiting refugees for direction, hopping on the endless caravan. But after miles of travelling, the stream turned to a trickle as families diverged east and west, heading to their hometowns. For Hong and his parents, though, they journeyed further south, as if they couldn't get far enough away from the communist advances. Pretty soon, they were on their own, relying for direction on the rising and setting of the sun.

Main roads, where communist units and tanks mobilised, were too dangerous, so they travelled through rougher, more mountainous terrain. Weeks of gruelling travel, driven by fear, left them spent and perpetually hungry. They finished their supplies long ago and had been subsisting on whatever Hong's mother could find. Watercress from lakes or streams, fern brakes and bitter nuts from forest floors, and berries from the hillside. In the last few days, their travels led them to a barren hillside where their tired, hungry bodies had reached the limit. There was nothing to forage and they had little energy to carry on.

The cooing mourning doves made Hong's stomach churn as he thought about meat. He imagined his mother's chicken soup, a whole game hen jostling in its broth. The savoury smell of meat infused with *jujubes*,[1] ginseng and sweet rice stuffed in the bird.

1 Dried red dates, also commonly known as Chinese red dates.

Hong could only let his imagination go so far. It was just too cruel to let himself think about the food he had left behind in Seoul. But since the communist invasion and the war, did anyone eat like that anymore? They marched along the hillside, ambling like drunks. When peeling birch bark looked tantalising enough to eat, it was time to get out of the wilderness. But the birds – actually, it was just the one magpie with a shiny wrapper in its beak that glinted and caught Hong's attention. It was their saviour. Hong and his parents stumbled down the hillside, following the magpie's flight path, and found the hidden village.

The villagers weren't surprised to see them; other refugees had wandered through. They took pity on Hong and his parents, and fed them some ground millet and watery bean sprout soup. It wasn't much of a meal, but Hong and his parents felt like royalty, and they slept that night in the soft comfort of a room, not a damp cave or a forest floor. They had been living like animals, and on their first night back in civilisation, they slept like babies.

But their luck didn't last too long. Early the next morning, they were awakened by South Korean soldiers scouring the countryside conscripting able-bodied men; twenty per village. The few men in this small village were old and not very able. The peasants' hollow eyes were fixed on Hong's father. "We'll take care of your boy and wife," a disembodied voice croaked. But Hong stepped up, and before anyone could do anything about it, one of the soldiers pulled him aside and led him out of the village.

Hong didn't even look back. His brothers weren't the only ones to show filial piety. He was 13 and able-bodied, and he didn't hesitate, though having a breakfast before he was taken would have been nice.

Hong was by far the youngest of the conscripts, and he quickly found himself near the back of the human train. It was still early morning and the birds were out. Magpies chittered from somewhere in the fields and an errant rooster's faint crow could be heard as they marched away from the village. Hong's hunger returned.

"I have a brother your age," said a voice behind him.

Hong looked over his shoulder. It was the rearguard soldier. He cradled the rifle like a tough soldier, but he was so willowy and thin that he swam in his uniform. If it wasn't for the belt cinched tightly around his loose green fatigues, he would have been nothing more than a clothes hanger. His army cap shaded his eyes, but not the weathered, stubbly face. Hong ventured the soldier was about 20, like his oldest brother.

"A bedwetter wouldn't have the guts you showed back there," the soldier said. "Hey, watch that side-eye, and face forward." He nudged his rifle against Hong's right shoulder.

Hong didn't want any trouble. He was out of his parents' care and he had no idea what the soldiers were capable of, but there was something about this young soldier that emboldened Hong.

"You could have at least let me say goodbye," Hong said, thinking about how he was pulled away so abruptly; and the missed breakfast, too.

"What was that? You need your mother to hold you?" the soldier mocked. "Maybe I was wrong. Maybe you are a bedwetter."

"I'm not a bedwetter!" Hong spat, but before he could turn his head to give him a stink eye, the barrel nudged his shoulder again.

"Easy," said the rearguard soldier. "What's your name?"

"Why do you care?"

"Now, that's not polite. You should respect your elders, Hong." Hong turned and gave him a stink eye, nudge or no nudge. "Step it up, kid," the soldier smiled and clicked his tongue.

* * *

The low hum of trucks and clouds of dust met them when they neared the army camp. In the midst of the loud chaos of the camp, Hong soon found himself with the other recruits standing at attention before an American officer. The man was much older than Hong's eldest brother. And he filled his uniform generously, unlike Rearguard who had nudged Hong all the way to the camp. The American inspected each conscript and interrogated them, with the aid of an interpreter who shadowed him. When the officer reached Hong, he shook his head at the interpreter. He said something in English and the interpreter looked chagrined.

"How old are you?" the interpreter asked Hong.

"Thirteen," he replied.

After the interpreter relayed Hong's answer, the officer examined Hong closely. He held up his hands, all ten fingers splayed, then he put eight fingers up. Hong understood what the officer was asking – Are you really 18?

Hong nodded.

The officer shook his head. Hong didn't get a rifle like the others; instead, he got a chocolate bar. The interpreter barked at him to go with the rest of the porters.

That night, Hong slept poorly in the porters' hut. His arms were sore from loading and unloading crates from the trucks. He wasn't used to carrying half his weight, even when he was decently fed. But it wasn't his muscles that ached and gave him trouble that night. It was his stomach.

Earlier in the day, the interpreter found him and tossed him a tin of corned beef. "Compliments of the Big Nose," the interpreter said and winked, "you have *noonchi*."[2]

---

2 A Korean word meaning a type of intuition that a person has from picking up subtle or non-verbal cues from a social situation.

Noonchi – not everyone has it, but when you're a third kid with older brothers, you learn to pick up on things that aren't said, Hong thought. Anyway, he didn't need to understand English to figure out the interpreter had lied about Hong's age, and he had no intention of making a fellow countryman lose face to a Big Nose.

But it was Hong who was losing more than his face now. For Hong, who hadn't had meat in more than six months, the tin of corned beef was a goldmine. He had never tasted canned meat. It was a luxury he wanted to savour, but he gave in to his hunger and the taste – oh, the amazing taste – and licked the tin clean. But now, the rich corned beef was finishing him off. Too fatty for his shrunken stomach, the corned beef kept him in the latrine most of the night. Hong lamented at the waste, but he took solace in the chocolate bar he had hidden in the lining of his jacket.

The days were long and he was learning the routine. Fill the jerrycans and load them into trucks. Unload rations from the trucks and reload with munitions and equipment. Keep the camp clean, sweep it for inspection.

He was also picking up a little English. He learned that the Big Nose soldiers were called "GIs".[3] He loved the GIs. These fresh-faced soldiers, full of optimism, were their liberators who had defeated Japan in the big war and kicked the Japanese occupiers out of Korea. And now, they'll do the same to the new invaders. The war would change the tide now that the GIs were fighting for the south. The Reds had no chance. How could they? The American GIs, so big and tall from all that canned meat, could easily beat the scrawny Red soldiers.

Hong also learned the word "kid" referred to him. He was the youngest in the camp and the GIs were always mussing his hair, like his brothers did, and they even helped him, like when he struggled to load a crate twice his weight into a truck.

3 An American English word meaning private soldier in the US Army.

"Don't let them help you," said Rearguard. He was back in the camp from scouring the remaining villages. "Be a man, bedwetter."

"Why do you care?"

"Again, 'why do you care?' Is that all you can say?" Rearguard shook his head. "Have some pride. Don't be their little mascot, all right?"

Hong gave him the stink eye.

"Listen, we're set to move. If you're a bedwetter, they'll leave you behind."

"No, they won't."

"Well, why do you think you're working in the camp? Do you see other porters sticking around here? They're moving supplies to the frontlines."

Hong hadn't considered what the other porters were doing. But he had *noonchi*, how could he have missed this? Truth be told, he was enjoying the attention from the GIs and the occasional treats. The GIs would sometimes toss him a "Charms", another word he learned. It was a hard piece of candy like marble that he could suck the sweetness out of until it dissolved. But then he thought about what Rearguard said and he didn't want to be a bedwetter.

"Where are they going?"

"North," said Rearguard.

"But it's swarming with Reds," Hong blurted, fear never really having left. The surprise invasion and the capture of their capital flashed across his mind. The mustard-uniformed soldiers and the churning tanks parading through the city gates of Seoul while Kim Il=sung's chilling voice blared through the loudspeaker, urging them to cheer for the liberators who came to vanquish the capitalists. Hong didn't understand politics, but he knew that the Reds came to torture and kill landowners like his parents. The Reds were monsters.

"The GIs are here, remember?" said Rearguard.

Of course, thought Hong. He remembered where he was and relief flowed through him. Of course, the big and well-fed GIs were strong enough to handle the Reds. Rearguard's optimism was contagious. It was a different story marching back north toward Seoul with a band of GIs compared to shambling along with his feeble old parents.

"Remember, pull your own weight," Rearguard said, clicking his tongue and mussing Hong's hair once again.

* * *

Hong still didn't get a weapon, instead he carried a backpack, a wooden A-frame pack filled with rolls of barbed wire. Hong didn't complain about the heavy load and he showed no sign of weakness, as Rearguard had advised him. He marched alongside a file of Korean soldiers, with Rearguard behind him and a trail of GIs that followed. A convoy truck rumbled before them. As they marched endlessly on the main road, Hong started daydreaming. He thought about his brothers and their reaction when he and the GIs rolled into Seoul. Their mouths would hang open in amazement. Their little brother coming back with the GIs, marching victoriously to recapture Seoul! Their eyes would bug out and they'd be weeping for joy, jumping up and down saying to their friends, "That's our little brother, Hong, the brave hero!"

Hong was smiling, foolishly oblivious of the whizzing noise that ended with a thud. A Korean soldier dropped in front of him, and a string of machine gun fire, *rat-a-tat-tat*, sang out from an invisible foe, causing the line of soldiers to break up into pandemonium.

Hong hit the ground, and before he knew it, he was crawling into a rice paddy. The cold water stung his shoulder where the barbs cut into him when he fell. He ducked under the shallow water. He waited there as long as his breath could last and until the muted sound of the firing rounds ceased. He raised his head, just barely. He was a frog, eyes above the water, scanning his surroundings. The bullets ceased, but his heart pounded just as loudly as it dawned on him that he was the only one in the rice paddy. The convoy of trucks and jeep remained deserted on the main road, and the GIs and South Korean soldiers were nowhere to be seen. He'd be a fool to run back to the trucks without the protection of the GIs. He'd be exposed. But he couldn't stay here all day, either. He had to move, but fear immobilised him, and he had no idea where to go.

A dragonfly skimmed the water above his sight line and he noticed a blur of olive green moving in the woods beyond the rice paddy. He slithered quietly through the murky shallow water, pushing through the stalks of rice that swayed jauntily as he passed. Soon, shots popped off and he froze as bullets whizzed past, hitting the water close to him. Hong thought he was a goner, but it was another bird that saved him. A large heron rose skyward from somewhere near him, and the shooting stopped.

Hong waited, holding his breath. Then a grenade exploded nearby, setting off a flurry of gunshots. In the mayhem, he got up and ran for the woods where he'd seen movement before. He knew that he could be running straight into the enemy, but he felt certain he'd seen the blur of GI-green, not the mustard colour of the enemy soldiers. Passing the first line of trees, he lurked, looking for cover, when a searing pain ripped through his shoulder as he felt his arm being pulled. He yelped. A hand immediately covered his mouth. It was Rearguard. The terror fled from Hong's eyes, and Rearguard released his hand from Hong's mouth. "Shhh." He held up a finger under his nose. Hong was all too glad to see his strange companion.

* * *

Hong blindly followed Rearguard. They were miles away from the main road and the convoy. The shadow lengthened to the left of the woods, so at least they were still headed north. They walked for miles in silence, away from the site of the ambush. When he was certain they were out of danger, Hong ventured to speak.

"We're lost, aren't we?"

"Not lost, just taking the scenic route," Rearguard said with a click of his tongue, again.

Hong's stomach grumbled. Hunger wasn't anything new, but the past few days of tinned meats had spoiled him, and getting reacquainted with that hollow pang in his stomach made him grumpy. Just when he was about to give up on Rearguard's lead, Hong heard a twig snap and Rearguard raised his hands up and said, "Hu-rend, hu-rend. GI, hu-rend."

A GI stood in front of them with a rifle trained on Rearguard. He regarded Rearguard suspiciously, but relaxed some when he saw Hong behind.

"Well, if it isn't the kid," said the GI, lowering his weapon.

He mussed Hong's hair and brought the two Koreans over to his camp. Three soldiers barely looked up from their digging, disappointed at what the scout had brought back. While some GIs were somewhat friendly, Hong had found others were not. Hong didn't need to know English to get the gist when they called him a "gook". The three in the camp were definitely not among the friendly GIs.

They made shelter for themselves and the GIs opened their cans of C-rations. The friendly one offered Hong a biscuit from his tin, but Rearguard,\ stuck his hand out in front of Hong, and Hong shook his head. The friendly GI shrugged his shoulder but tossed a Charms candy to Hong anyway. That night, Hong stuck close to Rearguard, and the two spent the night together in a small foxhole, barely large enough for them to squat. Hong gave up on food. His eyelids heavy with sleep. But Rearguard, by magic, pulled out three small orange balls.

"The bedwetter liked these," he said, peeling the tangerine skin. "Snot-nosed kid. He would have been your age."

"Would have?" Hong asked aloud. He should have known not to say the first thing on his mind. He had *noonchi*, after all. But Rearguard didn't seem to mind and continued peeling, even the white threads off the soft flesh.

"We were orphans," he said, offering Hong a perfect slice. "He would have been thirteen this year, except he was weak and got sick. If only he had food like the GIs', he might have had the strength …"

Hong felt his own pang for his family, especially his brothers.

"I don't even know your name," Hong said.

"Hyung," Rearguard said.

"Hyung?" Hong repeated incredulously. The literal word for brother? But Rearguard ignored it.

Then suddenly, he remembered what he always wanted to ask. "How did you know my name at the village?"

"I'm a fortune teller," Rearguard said with a click. "Nah, I heard your mother whispering to your father about Hong, the youngest. Now shut up and eat."

They ate in silence. Three tangerines, shared by the two, wasn't much of a meal but by the time he swallowed the last slice, Hong felt full. He didn't even think about the hard candy in his pocket.

* * *

Predawn, they were up with the chattering birds. Six of them marched through the thick woods, but Hong was confident the American GIs would reconnect with the rest of the troops by the end of the day, and he looked forward to the meal that awaited him at the camp. But by midday, it was clear that they were going around in circles. They treaded on alert for fear the Reds were lurking in the woods and eventually, they had to stop to refill their canteens. Hong shared Rearguard's water which helped dampen his hunger, somewhat.

It seemed to Hong that they were lost again, and though he and Rearguard followed the GIs blindly, they both wondered if the Americans knew what they were doing. The sun was starting its descent, and tempers were flaring. Hong heard a good share of "gook this" and "gook that" amongst the GIs. He had *noonchi* enough to figure out that the soldiers were frustrated and hungry as well.

For Hong, who had travelled with his parents through mountainous paths, this was familiar territory. He recalled his mother foraging, finding berries and bitter nuts. Now he found a forest floor littered with spiky balls. It stunk, but Rearguard said, "Ginko nuts!"

Pretty soon, they had a collection of the stinky, squishy balls in Rearguard's helmet. They brought it to share with the GIs, who squawked at the scent. But after Rearguard and Hong cleaned, hulled and roasted the nuts, the GIs didn't seem to complain.

They survived another day on tangerines and nuts, but with all the marching up and down the wooded mountain, the GIs were starting to flag in their spirits and energy. Big boned as they were, the GIs were accustomed to rich foods and were having trouble with just a handful of nuts and fruits. As they were making another weary ascent up a hill, the scout in the front put his right fist up and their march came to a halt. He pointed his weapon below and they saw smoke rising from a hamlet.

Hong understood the GIs intended to go into the hamlet. They looked battle-ready and hungry as if they thought the Reds might be hiding out there. But Hong was thinking of the small farming village where his parents remained with the frightened village women, children and old men. A thought came to him and he tugged on Rearguard's sleeve. It was worth a shot.

Rearguard spoke to the scout in his best English, which wasn't much, but with wild gesticulation and pointing, Rearguard somehow managed to get his point across. A string of English gibberish ensued and Hong picked out a few "gooks" and "kid" in a harsh, almost mocking tone. Rearguard said more words that sounded like Korean with an English lilt, and the GIs shrugged their shoulders and sighed. Eventually, Rearguard returned with his thumb sticking straight up – a "yes" sign he'd picked up from the GIs.

"We're going on your fowl hunt," he said, mussing Hong's hair.

Hong smiled, satisfied that his idea was a go. There would be no need to scare the villagers. Besides, they would be more cooperative if they weren't scared and knew they were helping their fellow countrymen. So, it was decided that Hong and Rearguard would reconnoitre the hamlet, ask for directions and maybe, procure a chicken for dinner. And no one would get hurt.

Hong's plan was brilliant and he was in high spirits, full of optimism heading down the hill.

"Hey, keep your guard up," said Rearguard, sobering the moment.

The hamlet was nothing more than a cluster of houses along a small lane. The largest house stood at the end, with a gate that swayed on its hinge. An uneasy feeling came over them as they walked cautiously down the desolate lane. They stopped at a house with a thatched roof, but it appeared vacant. In fact, most of the houses looked abandoned, with no sign of life, except for the one at the end with smoke rising from it. They heard a promising sound: an ox bellowing from behind the gate. Rearguard nudged the gate open with the butt of his rifle. In the middle of the courtyard, an old lady squatted near a brazier, fanning the flames.

"Granny, are you alone?" asked Rearguard, walking through the gate, looking around.

The old lady looked up. One of her eyes was clouded over and wandered while the other, the clear one, strained to make them out. She returned to her fire again, to burn the yellow and blood-soaked clothes.

"Granny," Hong tried, "Where is everyone?"

"Long gone," she said. "All fled before the Reds came through."

"They left you?" Hong asked incredulously.

She got up and limped over to the covered veranda. "I'd only slow everyone down. Anyway, I have everything I need here." As if on cue, the lowing ox sounded again.

Rearguard looked across the courtyard to the sheltered barn where the ox moaned. "Do you have any chickens?" he asked the old lady.

"I need eggs, don't I?" she said coolly.

Rearguard narrowed his eyes at her and she stared back, her good eye trained on him while her clouded one roved, giving an eerie and ominous look. Rearguard didn't hesitate, but swung the rifle off his shoulder and pointed it low and straight. He moved cautiously toward the barn.

It took a moment, but Hong had *noonchi* and picked up on Rearguard's meaning.

He made a move, but the old lady grasped Hong's arm, her clouded eye straining on him with meaning.

"Hyung!" Hong shouted. He was walking into a trap.

Hong tried to pull away, but the old lady was a lot stronger than she looked.

The ox bellowed and feathers flapped from inside the barn. There was a scuffle and the chickens squawked, spooked by the mayhem. There were thumps and groans, then a sudden crack, then silence. A long silence.

"Hyung!" Hong shouted again. The old lady released her iron grip and Hong ran toward the dark barn, toward Hyung.

When his eyes adjusted, Hong saw, a young boy, not much younger than himself, huddled by the ox. By the chicken coop, a man in peasant's clothes lay motionless at Rearguard's feet.

Rearguard held up a flapping chicken. "Take the chicken," he said.

Hong stared bewildered. The still man didn't look like a farmer. In fact, he looked like a young soldier disguised in old man's clothing.

"Did you kill him?" Hong asked.

"Take the chicken to the GIs," repeated Rearguard, thrusting the chicken forward. "You'll be fine." When Hong didn't answer, Rearguard dropped his weapon and wrung the chicken's neck. The bird jerked violently, then went limp. Hong was still, staring at the body lying on the hard-packed dirt floor.

"He was dying anyway, bleeding out," Rearguard said. "The old lady was burning his uniform. It was a mercy kill."

Hong dumbly took the lifeless chicken. "You're not coming?" But Hong knew even before he asked. Hong had *noonchi.* He understood without being told that the two Red deserters were hiding out in the old lady's barn. Hong had always thought the Reds were monsters, foes to be destroyed. But the dead boy in an old farmer's clothes and the little kid huddled in the corner were a mirror version of Rearguard and Hong. That sniffling, wide-eyed, shivering boy by the ox was the face of the enemy. And the enemy was not too different from himself.

Rearguard unbuttoned his olive military jacket, took it off and handed it to Hong, as he looked at the kid by the old white ox.

"What about you?" Hong asked.

"Tell them I went AWOL.[4] I've got to take care of this bedwetter," Rearguard said with a click.

4 An acronym for the military term "absent without official leave".

Hong was about to protest, but there was peace and finality in Rearguard's words. And Hong had enough *noonchi* to leave it alone.

Hong put on the too-large olive jacket and slung the rifle over his right shoulder. With the bird in his free hand, he marched toward the hill.

Author's Note

Writing historical fiction takes research. Fortunately, I love learning history. There are many parallels to draw from history that help me make sense of the current world. For instance, in the context of this story, how did North and South Korea come to be? I've read many non-fiction books and watched documentaries on the Korean War. While historians have helped me understand the political and social climate that led to the split in the nation, what had more impact and staying power were the stories of family members who had experienced the war. While their memories might be more muddled than the accuracy of facts and dates in a textbook, their experiences were real and authentic, and ultimately captured the essence of the Korean War.

It's important to capture human experience in historical fiction, otherwise, a textbook would serve just fine. This is not to say that historical fiction is only about the character – it is also about how the events in the past are essential in the journey and shaping of the character. In other words, the essential element is how this particular journey of the character could not have happened in any other time and place.

It may therefore sound like you would have to do a lot of research to write historical fiction, but there are no hard and-fast rules. Learn about the world you're building and mix in some imagination. So long as you remain authentic to the world and to the character, you'll have a story that will engage the reader.

The Cassette

Prasanthi Ram

The majority of Singaporeans and residents of Singapore live in government-subsidised public housing known as Housing and Development Board (HDB) flats. The HDB is a statutory board that is responsible for the iconic high-rise flats that define the city's heartlands. Here, people of all walks of life and cultural backgrounds coexist.

The *karang guni* man used to be a familiar sight within HDB neighbourhoods, particularly in the 1980s and 1990s. The term itself comes from Malay, meaning "gunny sack". Essentially a rag-and-bone man, he would announce his presence with a loud rubber horn and go from door to door collecting recyclables such as newspapers and used (sometimes even damaged) electronics like television sets and radios from residents in exchange for cash. It should be noted that while *karang guni* men frequented HDB estates, they were not permitted to conduct business around private housing such as condominiums or landed properties. Although there are still *karang guni* men around today, it is a dying trade, especially with the onset of the digital age and evolving market conditions. For many Singaporeans, they continue to represent a nostalgic slice of the past.

1999

On Tuesday evenings, the *karang guni* man comes to Keerthana's part of the neighbourhood.

His weekly visit is one of the few things that gets her genuinely excited, alongside late-night red bean *potong*[1] ice cream from the tricycle-carted ice-cream seller and the eclectic 50-cent capsule toys from the vending machines at the neighbourhood market. Whenever the rag-and-bone man makes his festive entrance at the outdoor carpark below her HDB block, she finds herself dancing

1 Cut in Malay, in this context it refers to the "cut" pieces of local ice cream sold on sticks.

on her tippy-toes, each step matched to the addictive offbeat rhythm of his horn in a way that would make her *bharatanatyam*[2] teacher proud.

Her mother, too, looks forward to the Tuesday flash sales by their front gate. On a shoestring budget at home, *Amma*[3] recycles anything and everything. All the ice-cream boxes and butter cookie tins around the house are unfailingly repurposed into containers for sewing supplies and unlabelled cooking powders that only she can tell apart, much to the chagrin of her dessert-loving children. *Amma* also sets aside items that she thinks can be sold off to the *karang guni* man for quick money – mostly the morning papers. In fact, she is so committed that one corner of their balcony is dedicated solely to old newspapers, *The Straits Times* and *Tamil Murasu*, sometimes even *The New Paper* and old *Anantha Vikadan* magazines sneakily hidden within. Usually, after *Appa*[4] is done reading the papers, *Amma* pulls out a few pages to wrap stalks of coriander and curry leaves, and then a few more to clean glass surfaces around the house. But the remainder always goes into the towering corner pile, and Keerthana, wanting to be like her mother in every way possible, appoints herself in charge of it.

Today, *Amma* has something more lucrative to offer on top of the usual newspaper stack worth a dollar. It is her radio cassette player that was a gift from her parents in Kalakad years ago. Keerthana is thrilled as she imagines how many more dollar coins it will earn.

"Will Uncle take this?" she asks *Amma*, as she reverently traces the edges of the radio to the tip of its thin metal antenna.

"I hope so," *Amma* replies in Tamil. "I haven't used it in a while. May as well sell it and make some money."

2 Traditional classical Indian dance.
3 Mother in Tamil.
4 Father in Tamil.

It is around a quarter to five that she hears the familiar rubber horn along with a catchy tune belted out by a strong pair of lungs: "*Karang guni! Siu bo zhua, pai laydio, dian si ki,*" each vowel dragging longer than the one before, interspersed with rhythmic honks that are in strained harmony with the cuckooing koels of the evening. She does not know what any of the words mean. It will only be years later that she discovers the words are in fact Hokkien for "collecting newspapers, damaged radios, television sets". But it does not matter. She has heard it so many times that her mouth moves on its own volition to mimic each strange sound. It is a mere act of approximation and she is aware that most of her version is wrong, but the attempt had her keeling over in peals of laughter as she dances along to his seasoned performance.

Unceremoniously, *Amma* slides open the carpark-facing window to shout for his attention: "Uncle! Here, here!" The horn halts, as if in recognition of her equally competent lung capacity, before it resumes its easy ruckus towards their block. Keerthana is already kneeling at the grilled gate, peering nose first into the corridor in anticipation of his arrival. He usually takes the stairs to their second-storey flat as it is faster that way. In the end, it takes him a total of 20 minutes, by which time she is perspiring and leaning against *Amma*'s stack of newspapers which reaches up to her shoulder.

"*Thangachi, saaptiya?*" He greets *Amma* jovially just as he always does, pushing his blue industrial trolley in front of him. The trolley already has a stack of newspaper on it, as well as a thick coil of pink raffia string and a handheld spring scale hanging on the handle.

His Tamil greeting of "Little sister, have you eaten?" is a tongue-in-cheek alternative to the usual "hello" that makes Keerthana feel seen and appreciated, unlike the racial slurs that had been thrown her way since kindergarten.

Amma cringes though, probably because of his frivolous butchering of her native tongue, but she still manages a gracious smile. She is certainly an admirable businesswoman. "Hello, Uncle. Today we have more than just newspaper," she says, handing over the stack.

He secures the stack with raffia string, and deftly cuts the end from the coil with a penknife before pulling both ends into a knot. Hooking the tied stack with the small scale, he lifts the whole bundle. Keerthana is not so good with big numbers but even she can tell the weight is worth a dollar indeed. With a lopsided smile, he drops the stack onto the trolley and says, "Always correct. What you have for me?"

"Cassette radio." *Amma* presents the prized item for his assessment. He takes it into his skinny, tanned hands, cradling it like one might a newborn infant.

"*Thangachi*, old model. People use CD now, you know."

"I know," Amma replies, slightly haughty. "That's why I sell to you."

The *karang guni* man laughs, revealing his missing incisor. He tongues the exposed gum before asking, "Working or not?"

"Everything works except for the record button. You can check. It's in good condition."

"It's okay. I trust you. Five dollars."

"Only five? Give me a better price!"

"Better price!" Keerthana echoes her mother's bargaining, stomping her foot the way her *bharatanatyam* teacher taught her, just to pressure him further.

"Okay, okay, six. Just for you," the *karang guni* man says with a dramatic sigh, wagging a finger at her.

After securing the radio cassette player and the newspapers in place with raffia, he pulls out three $2 notes and a single gold coin from his waist pouch. Keerthana's jaw drops because in her short career of assisting *Amma* with these transactions, only coins have been part of the exchanges. She glances up at *Amma* just as her mother looks down at her and they both exchange secret smiles; this is, without a doubt, a business milestone. When the rag-and-bone man rattles off in the direction of their neighbour Auntie Yasmin's flat, *Amma* presses the coin into Keerthana's palm and says, like a master to her apprentice, "You've earned it."

* * *

When Tuesday afternoon arrives again the following week, she is giddy from a fun morning at school. She inspects the corner pile and starts pulling off the newspapers from the top to make a dollar stack. In her eagerness, about $1.50 worth of newspapers topple over her tiny body. It is a disaster. But she wilfully takes it in her stride. She is her mother's apprentice and she has a reputation to maintain. *Remember when you had a bad fall at the courtyard during recess hopscotch but did not cry? Yes, you are that kid.* So, she diligently completes her stack, stands atop it, and piles the rest precariously back onto the corner pile.

But strangely, *Amma* has not mentioned the *karang guni* man at all today. In fact, she has been seated beside the landline phone for the past ten minutes, copying a complicated series of numbers from the back of a calling card onto a letter pad, adding more numbers to the list, then dials them all in order. From the look of her deeply furrowed brows, Keerthana is afraid to interrupt her to ask about today's sale. Instead, the girl quietly takes apart the stack into thirds, and shakily transports them from the balcony to the front door over three trips. When *Amma* sees this later, she will be impressed enough to reward her effort with another coin for her piggy bank.

When the *karang guni* song begins just on time as expected, echoing upwards from the open carpark, *Amma* slams the receiver down against the phone table, charges towards the windows and pulls them shut. As they quiver against the grilles from the impact, she locks them for good measure; the loud clicks hide the little gasp that escapes from Keerthana. Then *Amma* charges back to restart on her numbers again, but not without a groan of frustration first. Coming to her rescue, the landline rings at that moment, its sound cascading crudely over the muffled sound of the rubber horn.

Whoever is on the other line compels *Amma* to collapse into a breathless outpouring in Tamil: "I've been trying to call you all day. Why aren't you at home?" But the rest of it is lost on Keerthana as *Amma* rambles on too fast, her words tinged with a native Brahmin twang. What Keerthana notices though, with her back pressed against the closed front door, is this: as *Amma* urgently tries to articulate her emotions, her mouth trembles between words, her eyes mist over, and her idle hand begins to shake against her knees. It is clear as day – something is wrong.

Before Keerthana can figure out what had happened, the doorbell rings.

She knows very well not to open the door for strangers. It has, after all, been drilled into her ever since she spoke her first words. But *Amma*, too preoccupied with her phone call, does not seem to have registered that someone is outside. The girl presses her ear against the door for some aural clue as to who it may be. Sadly, the wood does not reply. Defeated, she slumps against it, wishing she were tall enough to look through the peephole that the adults use, but her eyes are only level with the doorknob. Then she hears it, the rubber horn directly behind her – one singular honk as if in casual greeting.

With as much finesse as she can muster, she silently turns the knob and slides out into the small space between the door and the metal gate. The *karang guni* man is indeed outside, with streams of perspiration down his neck and the same blue trolley in front of him. But it is already full with all kinds of things and she is sure he will not be able to take more newspapers even if she asks. She wonders why he is here at all.

"Where's your mother?"

She presses an index finger to her lips as if to silence him. "Mummy is crying," she whispers.

The man looks taken aback at her answer, then nods slowly as he processes it. "*Oi*, you cannot anyhow open the door for people, *leh*. What if a bad person comes?"

"But I know it's you!"

He shakes his head left and right in a slow dramatic fashion to show his disapproval but cannot hide the small smile that flickers on his weathered face.

"Tell your mother, this is hers." He removes a cassette tape from his waist pouch and pushes it through a gap between the metal grills of the gate. She takes it in her hands and looks at the item that has been labelled in a language she cannot read. She flips it back and forth between the two sides, feeling perplexed. *Is it not the job of the* karang guni *man to collect old items, not the other way around?*

"Uncle, we have many cassette tapes at home. We don't need this."

He clicks his tongue, as if she has just said the most idiotic thing. "*Aiyah*, I found this inside the radio cassette player she gave me last week. It's your mother's. So, give it back to her, okay? Go, go." He shoos her off. "Go inside."

Holding the cassette tape to her chest, she gingerly slides back into the flat. The soft thud of the closing wooden door almost gives her away, except *Amma* is no longer at the telephone table. The door to the prayer room is shut. *Amma* has probably started her usual sunset mantras and only a fool would dare to interrupt her.

As quietly as possible, Keerthana tiptoes past the sacred room, then races to the television console in the living room, where her family's one and only radio cassette player sits. It is a silver Philips giant that plays both CDs and cassettes, and lights up in the centre display. She presses the eject button, slots her newly acquired cassette into the open compartment with its "B" side facing up, and closes it. Then, with a deep breath, she hits the play button.

From the speakers booms a woman's voice. She is chanting mantras that sound quite like the ones *Amma* recites daily within the sanctity of her prayer room for Goddess Lalitha Devi. The voice is hypnotic and firm but with reasonable gravel that betrays her age. *Who is she?* But Keerthana's latent curiosity is quickly overshadowed by panic. It is much too loud, and *Amma* will be furious if she is disturbed during her prayers. The girl begins tapping the volume button on the player, but she has clumsily mistaken the plus sign for the minus, and the mantras begin to fill her little head, the sound enveloping her like the cling wrap *Amma* uses to pack *Appa*'s chapati rolls.

Suddenly, a man's throaty chuckle, as if from a distance, emanates from the tape and the woman breaks her chanting to chide him. "Keep quiet, *Mama*![5] I'm doing this so that Padma can learn the mantras," she hears the woman on the cassette tape croak in Tamil. With a yelp, she scrambles to push down on the minus button until and finally the volume is at its lowest. She can barely celebrate her relief though because from a distance, a door clicks open.

Without turning to look over her shoulder, she already knows that *Amma* is walking towards her, her *thali*[6] and all the extra

5 Term of address in Tamil with several meanings, commonly used to refer to uncle, also used by women to address their husbands as a term of endearment.

6 A sacred gold thread or chain that is worn by a married Hindu woman.

safety pins she has attached to the long matrimonial chain jangling menacingly against her chest. Maybe it is too late for Keerthana to dissociate herself from the act. But she gets to her feet and slowly backs away from the radio.

"What is that?"

Keerthana winces. When she finally looks up at *Amma*, she sees that her mother's eyes are red. "The *karang guni* man," she starts slowly.

"What?" *Amma* snaps. "Speak louder."

She clears her throat and half-shouts. "The *karang guni* man gave me this cassette tape. He said he found it. In the radio we gave last week. Sorry." She bows her head.

Pushing Keerthana aside, *Amma* kneels before the radio, as if about to lay prostrate in prayer. When she increases the volume again, the man in the recording seems to have left because the woman has resumed her mantras. Frowning, as if this is not what she wishes to hear, *Amma* pauses the cassette, hits the reverse button, waits for the tape to circle backwards for a few seconds, and then presses the play button. There, the laugh! There, they are arguing! The mantras! *Amma* does it all again: pause, reverse, play and again. And then, once more.

By her tenth listen, *Appa* and Krishnan, Keerthana's older brother, are home. The girl further distances herself, hiding behind the sofa, afraid. Afraid that she may be scolded by her mother. Afraid that *Amma* may be losing her mind. Afraid that *Appa* will blame her for opening the door in the first place.

But neither of them notices her fear or seems to care.

"*Ennanga*,"[7]Amma calls out in Tamil, brokenly. Almost immediately, *Appa* drops his briefcase onto the floor where his leather shoes have been divested and strides over to her. He, too, is on his knees now, and he pulls her into his arms, her head cradled under his chin. "That's his voice. I haven't heard it in so long,"

7 A respectful term of address in Tamil that wives use to call their husbands.

she cries against his neck, her whole body crumpling into his. He holds her tight, then rocks her back and forth. Pause, reverse, play. "He's as good as dead now. *Appa*'s as good as gone."

It is then that Keerthana has an epiphany – or at least, an almost-epiphany. It emerges as a blur at first, a garble of emotions that settles heavily upon her chest, yet to fully develop.

She will only be able to articulate it when she becomes an adult, after she understands that "as good as gone" means to be alive yet forever asleep, a deadweight on a hospital bed with tubes connected up to veins and a brain that has quit before managing last words to beloved daughters far away in a distant country. One day, when she drives around her old neighbourhood for nostalgia's sake and hears the distant horn of a disappearing legend by pure chance, she will reminisce and think: the *karang guni* man collects more than just old newspapers, broken radios and television sets. Grief, too, sits on that blue trolley of his, between paper and raffia. And, sometimes, grief looks like that cassette filled with hidden sounds etched onto a thin magnetic strip, from a man who died oceans away, and for a woman who mourns her father for the rest of her years.

Right now, though, Keerthana's first order of business is not to cry for the grandfather she does not know, the widowed grandmother she will grow to know, or her iron-willed *Amma* who weeps before her for the first time. It is not even to unpack that blurred, garbled epiphany that weighs her down with discomfort since her tongue is not yet accustomed to the language of loss and grief. Instead, it is to move that golden coin from the *karang guni* man into the gap behind the bottom drawer of the cupboard in her bedroom. Far away from her line of sight, just like her only grandparents. Her "as good as gone" grandfather. She never reaches for that drawer anyway. So, she will soon forget that the dollar is lurking there. She will even forget about most of that Tuesday evening. And after her father gets promoted at work, she and her family will move out to a more befitting home in a condominium, where the voices of *karang guni* men cannot be heard. Only the coin will remain in a flat of emptied rooms, as an untouched, steadfast emblem covered in dust and sometimes creepy crawlies. Eventually, that cupboard and its secret space will also be torn down from the walls, for a new family, their new home, and at some point, their new grief.

Author's Note

The maternal side of my family is based entirely in India. As I grew up in an era that preceded Skype and WhatsApp, I was unable to establish a close relationship with my grandparents, unlike friends at school. I knew what they looked like and how they sounded but it was more a factual understanding than a sign of an established emotional bond. This also meant that my first experience of loss and grief was at a distance. When my grandfather passed away, I was numb and incapable of processing my mother's outward grief. It was only a week later upon seeing a photograph of him holding me as a baby that I realised I had indeed lost someone so integral to my mother's and my existence. While I was 16 when this happened, unlike Keerthana who is much younger in this story, grief made me feel the same way as she does in the narrative: like a lost child.

A large part of the story focuses on the relationship between Keerthana and the *karang guni* man because he is the closest to a grandfather she will ever have. There is an inherent innocence between them: he, as an elderly person, cares for her safety while she, a child who has grown up looking forward to his visits, trusts him enough to share a secret. Even if the *karang guni* man seems like a supporting cast member in this narrative, he in fact plays the important role of a catalyst in the final revelation. It is because he returns the cassette that *Amma* hears her father's voice again. Seeing her otherwise tenacious mother break down is a crucial moment in young Keerthana's life, who realises firsthand what family can mean despite distance.

One strategy when writing a story is to divert your reader's attention from the main event, only to lead them back without their realisation. A story about loss does not have to begin with loss; in fact, it does not have to end with loss, either. What the protagonist chooses to focus on, the newspaper stacks, the *karang guni* man or the dollar coin, can say much more about the loss than an author explicitly spelling it out.

About the Writers

Clara Mok loves reminiscing about her childhood and wishes to capture snippets of Singapore's past before they disappear. She is eternally thankful to Writing the City's "Write-in Sessions" for the platform which allowed her story "The Newspaper Phantom" to germinate and blossom. Clara graduated from Nanyang Technological University, Singapore. She was selected for the Mentor Access Project 2016/17 by the National Arts Council in Singapore. Her short stories have been published in *Writing the City – Fresh Fiction from Singapore* and online literary publications. She is an English educator and shares her love for writing with her students.

Carol Pang recently completed a two-year MA in English Literature at Uppsala University, Sweden. She holds a BA (first class honours) in English Literature from The Open University, UK. She has published and won prizes for several of her short stories and creative non-fiction pieces. She won first prize in the 2020 Short Story Competition by *Bengaluru Review*, third prize in the 2019 short story contest by *Ergo* (the Uppsala Student Union newspaper) and second prize in the New Asian Writing Short Story Competition 2016. She was also awarded the competitive editorial mentorship by the online literary journal, *Gordon Square Review*. She can be found online at https://www.linkedin.com/in/carolyhpang.

Karen Kao is the author of *The Dancing Girl and the Turtle* (Linen Press, 2017), her debut novel set in 1930s Shanghai. Her short form fiction and essays have been published in *The Habtic Standard* (the Netherlands), *The Common* (US), *The Shanghai Literary Review* (China), *Nunum* (Canada) and *Cha* (Hong Kong), among others. Her work has been nominated for the Pushcart Prize, the VERA and the

Best of the Net. Karen teaches creative writing at the International Writers' Collective in Amsterdam, the Netherlands. She is currently at work on more projects than she can keep track of. Mrs Yip is a character in her next novel, a sequel to *The Dancing Girl and the Turtle.*

Lalaine F Yanilla Aquino is a professor in the Department of English and Comparative Literature, College of Arts and Letters, University of the Philippines (UP) Diliman. She teaches creative writing, stylistics, children's literature, literacy, translation studies and language studies among other courses at the undergraduate and graduate levels. She has been awarded the ONE UP Professorial Chair, the UP Centennial Professorial Chair and the UP International Publication Award. Her research articles have been included in books and anthologies published by Routledge, Palgrave Macmillan, Gale Cengage and Multilingual Matters. Her dissertation on the effect of bilingual instruction on children's literacy skills was awarded the most outstanding research at the doctoral level by the UP College of Education and the Department of Science and Technology.

Debasree Ghosh is currently pursuing her PhD in English Literature at Victoria University of Wellington, New Zealand. She was born in Kolkata and educated at Calcutta International School, and subsequently attended the Jadavpur University Department of English, where she completed her Bachelor's and Master's degrees in English Literature. In 2011, she received a Ministry of Education scholarship from the Singapore government to pursue a Postgraduate Diploma in Education from the National Institute of Education, upon completion of which she taught General Paper at Anglo-Chinese Junior College. She has been a creative writing facilitator at The Creative Arts Institute in Kolkata as well as an International Baccalaureate Diploma programme teacher in Delhi NCR, before she moved to Wellington. She currently resides in Wellington with her family.

Ismim Putera is a writer from Sarawak, Malaysian Borneo. His works have appeared in numerous online literary journals and are also forthcoming in *Men Matters Online, A Thousand Cranes Poetry Anthology* and *Lyric: A Speculative Poetry Anthology*. His debut poetry chapbook is *Tide of Time* (Mug and Paper Publishing, 2021).

Alice Bianchi-Clark is Italian by nationality. She has lived and worked in Rome, London, Paris, Beijing and Hong Kong. Having studied Modern Chinese Studies at Trinity Hall, Cambridge, she has been drawn to Asia ever since. She currently resides in Singapore. Alice's short stories: "The Biker Jacket" was a winner of the *Elle Magazine* short story competition in 2013, "Rosemary" was published in the *Quarterly Literary Review Singapore* in 2015 and "The Ribbon Girl" was published in an anthology for children entitled *A Book of Hugs* (2020). Alice is a multilingual performance storyteller with festival experience in Singapore, Malaysia and India. She is also a freelance journalist, children's educator and member of the Society of Children's Book Writers and Illustrators.

Heidi Emily Eusebio-Abad used to teach creative writing courses in the University of the Philippines and is an award-winning author of children's books in the Philippines. Her first book, *Abot Mo Ba ang Tainga Mo? (Can You Reach Your Ear?)*, won the 2002 Gintong Aklat Award for Children's Literature, while *Polliwog's Wiggle* was a finalist in 2006. Her collection of poems titled *Child of Earth* won Second Prize in the 2009 Carlos Palanca Memorial Awards for Children's Literature. Her recent books cater to specific advocacies: *Water Lilies for Marawi* is used in a reading-as-therapy programme for the children of Marawi displaced during the city's siege; *Kung Ako'y Isa (If I Were)* educates children about the dangers of dengue and what they can do to avoid contracting this deadly fever; *Dr Dapdap: The Healing Tree* introduces children to the endemic trees of the Philippines.

Sohana Manzoor is an Associate Professor at the Department of English and Humanities at University of Liberal Arts Bangladesh. She has a PhD from Southern Illinois University Carbondale and her area of expertise is 19th-century British literature. Her short stories, non-fiction works and translations have been published in *The Dhaka Tribune, The Daily Star, Bengal Lights* and *Six Seasons Review.* In 2020, one of her short stories was accepted for publication in the web edition of *The Best Asian Short Stories.* She is currently the literary editor of *The Daily Star* in Bangladesh.

Sumitra Selvaraj is a writer and media professional who lives in Malaysia. Sumitra was the executive producer of a television talk show which ran for over 850 episodes in Malaysia and Singapore. In 2019, she took on a six-month contract as a producer and presenter with BFM Radio. She began writing creative fiction in 2016 and was runner-up at the 2016 DK Dutt Memorial Prize for Literary Excellence. She won the 2018 Short Story Prize at the Asian Women Writers Festival in Singapore, and her work has appeared in the short story anthologies *Remang, Endings & Beginnings* and *The Principal Girl*, as well as in online platforms *Rambutan Literary*, *Anak Sastera* and *Malaysian Indian Anthology*. She is also the founder of Sarees and Stories, an Instagram platform where she documents her daily drape.

Tina Jimin Walton is a Korean-American writer in Singapore. She loves stories that empower and encourage youth and writes what her younger self would have liked to read. She has an MFA in Creative Writing from Vermont College of Fine Arts (2016), a BA in Economics and Japanese Studies from University of California, Berkeley, and an MA in Economics from University of Washington. *Last Days of the Morning Calm* is her first novel, a historical fiction work for young adults. It was shortlisted for the 2018 Scholastic

Asian Book Award. Her short story, "Short and Sweet", can be found in *A Book of Hugs* (2020), an anthology for young readers. You can keep up with her on her website: www.tinajiminwalton.com.

Prasanthi Ram is a PhD candidate for Creative Writing at Nanyang Technological University, Singapore, and has an MA in Creative Writing from the University of Sydney. "The Cassette" is from a larger collection of connected short stories forming part of her PhD dissertation. Her fiction works have been published in *The Tiger Moth Review* , *The Willowherb Review*, as well as *Food Republic: A Singapore Literary Banquet* (Landmark Books, 2020). Outside of fiction, she is a regular reviewer and essay reader for *Singapore Unbound*'s "SP Blog". She co-founded and is the fiction editor of *Mahogany Journal*, an online literary journal dedicated to South Asian writers born or based in Singapore.

About the Editor

Anitha Devi Pillai (PhD) has authored and edited creative and non-creative fiction books as well as translated a historical fiction novel, *Sembawang: A Novel* (2020) from Tamil into English. She also loves writing poetry, some of which have made their way into the classrooms in Singapore, India, Australia, and the Philippines. Many of her works explore themes such as identity, heritage, and culture.

She is best known for her research into the Singapore Malayalee community that was supported by a National Heritage Board (Singapore) grant and resulted in the publication of *From Kerala to Singapore: Voices from the Singapore Malayalee Community* (2017) For this study, Anitha was awarded a 'Pravasi Express Research Excellence Award' in 2017.

Her other books are *Project Work: Exploring Processes, Practices and Strategies* (2008), *From Estate to Embassy: Memories of an Ambassador* (2019), A *View of Stars: Stories of Love* (2020), and *The Story of Onam* (in press).

Anitha's favourite genres to write are the short story and creative non-fiction prose. Her stories have appeared in various anthologies including *The Best Asian Short Stories 2019*, *Letter to my Son* (2020) and *Food Republic: A Singapore Literary Banquet* (2020). She is currently writing a collection of short stories focusing on food and love.

In a parallel life, she is an applied linguist and teacher educator at the National Institute of Education (NIE), Nanyang Technological University (NTU), Singapore where she teaches courses on various forms of writing and trains English language teachers to teach writing. Anitha is a three-time recipient of teaching awards: 'Excellence in Teaching Commendation Award' from NIE, NTU in 2018 and the 'SUSS Teaching Merit Award' in 2014 and 2013 from the Singapore University of Social Sciences.